SPENT LIVES

SPENT LIVES

Stories by
Martin Itzkowitz

Printed in the United States.

Cover and book design by Asya Blue Design.

ISBN 979-8-9901881-4-3 Hardcover Casebound
ISBN 979-8-9901881-5-0 Paperback
ISBN 979-8-9901881-6-7 Ebook

for Ann
(with whom I've spent mine)

CONTENTS

A NOTE ON WORDS
FROM YIDDISH AND HEBREW

Words transliterated from Yiddish, Hebrew, and Aramaic (in one instance) occur in all but two of the stories in this collection. I have appended a glossary for most of them. However, when meanings of such words are apparent from their contexts (immediate or within a few sentences preceding or following) no further definition is required.

In one story, where Yiddish and Hebrew are somewhat plentiful and sometimes involve complete sentences, translations typically appear in brackets. A few words, whether here or elsewhere, for various reasons not defined at once, are nevertheless included in the glossary.

In three instances, I have used Hebrew characters. The second and third of these are transliterations and are followed in the text by their English originals. The first, כשר, is the Hebrew word that translates as "kosher."

Transliterations both for Yiddish and Hebrew spoken by the characters follow (with occasional minor variations) the method for Yiddish prescribed by the YIVO Institute for Jewish Research. In this system, each letter (or cluster representing a specific sound) is pronounced. For example, the word *bobe* (grandmother) contains two syllables, rather than one, which a speaker of English might expect.

There are occasional exceptions. Names, whether actual or fictional (if likely for time, place, or condition) are not transliterated. For example, because the spelling of *Etz* and

Chaim in the synagogue named Etz Chaim (Tree of Life) is in all likelihood how it would have appeared on the building and its documents, I have kept it here. For a similar reason, I have retained the prevailing spelling of author Sholem Aleichem's surname.

In addition, words in Hebrew and Yiddish, particularly those involving religious observances and practice, assumed to be quite familiar to most readers through prevailing American orthographic practice (e.g., Yom Kippur and Bar Mitzvah), might not be transliterated. This has been decided on a case-by-case basis, determined largely by such matters as my perception of a character's age, background, and the time frame in which the action occurs. In a given story, the same character might at times use Yiddish or Hebrew words in their usual English (non-Yivo) rendering while using Yivo versions at others. In general, characters are assumed to be of Ashkenazic origin and essentially unaffected by Modern Hebrew pronunciation.

Passages written in the narrator's voice use prevailing American spelling exclusively.

KEY TO PRONUNCIATION

Vowels

a=the vowel in *far, fog*/ ***e***=the vowel in *bet, wren*
i=ranges from the vowel in *fish* to that of *feet*
o=the vowel in *hub, hovel*
u=ranges from the vowel in *put* to the vowel *in soon*

Diphthongs

ay=he diphthong in *mild, shy*/***ey***=the diphthong in *shade,
convey* ***oy***=the diphthong in *coil, joy*, (approximate)

Consonants

Consonants are typically pronounced as they are in English.
However, *g* is restricted to its "hard" form as in *go* and *gag* and
the letters *c, j, q, w,* and *x* are never used.

kh=the consonant cluster in *Bach*/**dzh**=the *g* in *gem*
ts=the consonant cluster in *cats, blitz*
tsh=the consonant cluster in *chip, watch*/ **zh**=the s in pleasure

Note: Final letters of some clusters, as in *mazl* (luck) and
mameloshn, (mother tongue, i.e., Yiddish) have syllabic value.

The Lives

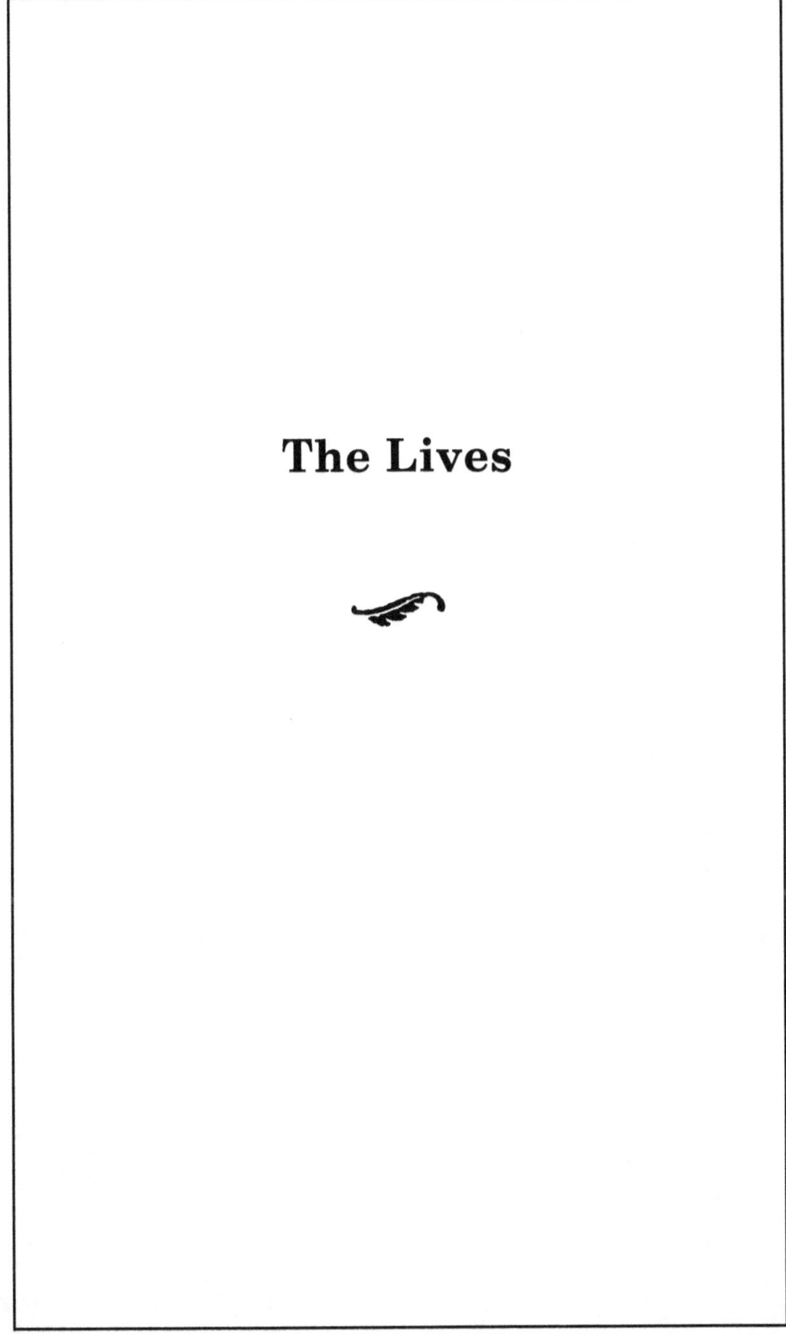

Vendetta

On a chill autumn morning, Arthur Adler stood atop the steps of his fashionable Brooklyn brownstone and adjusted the velvet collar of his Chesterfield coat. The garment struck the one assertive note in his conservative business dress of dark three-piece suit, off-white shirt, and muted striped tie, although both the coat and the collar itself were gray. He paused to survey the quiet cat-chic street. Indeed, on the sand-colored sills of several looming windows Siamese and Persians, a déclassé rescue or two, and an odd Angora had already curled themselves to catch the early sun. Split-leaved philodendrons or avocados grown from pits reserved from some primordial guacamole arched above them, completing the miniature Rousseauvian jungle scene. Still, on the walls behind, a framed poster, an unframed abstract painting, or hand-loomed tapestry suggested accessible civilization and urbanity within reach.

Satisfied with his mastery, or, at least, stewardship over all he beheld, Adler looked at his watch. It was 7:33 and he had planned to be at his desk at Weeks and Loew by 8:00, well before the market's opening. He reached for the brown calfskin briefcase at his feet, took three quick steps, started, slowed taking two more, then halted altogether.

"I don't believe it," he muttered to himself. "In this day and age. At this hour. Here!"

He resumed his descent mechanically, shaking his head as if to clear his vision as he went. Reaching the sidewalk, he stopped again.

"I don't believe it," he repeated aloud.

Then, in slight arc and with short, shuffling steps as if approaching a UFO just landed, Adler made his hesitant way toward the object of his disbelief.

It was a small, closed metal cart on rubber wheels covered with a silver paint whose glare illuminated the black legend on its front and sides—Bubbe's כּשׂר Knishes. At the rear of the cart, hands in pockets, chin on chest, a man sat hunched and dozing on a wooden crate once used to carry bottled milk. His broad-billed cap concealed his face in shadow, though, even with the earlaps down, his lobes were exposed and red. Beneath a yellowed and stained apron, he wore a tattered khaki coat, army surplus of indeterminate vintage. His sturdy black twill trousers, adorned with grease spots, were tucked into worn, formerly thick-soled boots.

Sensing someone's presence, the seated man raised his head, smiled, and looked steadily at Adler with surprisingly lively blue eyes. Taken aback once more, Adler retreated a step or two and leaned against his wrought iron fence.

"Harvey?" he gasped. "Is it you Harvey Kimmelman?"

Kimmelman raised a confirming eyebrow.

"What are you doing here? What is all this? Halloween's over you know, "Adler jested, his laugh a punctured balloon deflating as he spoke. He fumbled for his handkerchief and dabbed at his brow.

"And Purim's coming. So, who's in costume?" Kimmelman replied. "I'm here to sell you a knish. Cheap."

He pointed to one of the cardboard placards at the corners of the cart where, followed by a cent sign, the figure 6 was superimposed over the original 5.

"At seven-thirty in the morning? You've got to be kidding. Besides, I've had breakfast. Knishes and croissants don't mix."

Kimmelman nodded.

"My point exactly."

"Listen, Harv," Adler began, confidential though lacking confidence. "This has got to be some kind of joke, right? And it's funny—I guess. But I've really got to get to the office."

"All right. Take a knish for your coffee break."

"What? No. I couldn't. Where—where would I put it?"

Kimmelman glanced toward the briefcase.

Adler clutched it to his chest.

Kimmelman shrugged.

"But what about you?" Adler resumed, as if taking heart from the embrace. "Aren't you still with the welfare department?"

"Nights."

"Nights?"

"Sure nights. It's the best time. Electronics come out of the closet, jewelry comes out of the drawer, husbands and lovers come out of the sofa beds. Nights—if you're into welfare and fraud among the poor. Daytimes . . ."

Kimmelman spread his arms as if to include both Adler and the street.

"You're crazy, insane—m—m—"

"Meshuge."

"Mentally deranged," Adler snapped.

He turned and strode off toward the subway but stopped after a few paces and turned back. He was in control now, almost jaunty as he approached Kimmelman again.

"It's revenge, isn't it?"

"Revenge?"

"For last month when I beat you at Chinese. But I always

beat you at Chinese—when we were little kids in Brownsville, when we were bigger kids in Flatbush—and last month—we were drunk—and even then I beat you. Harv, I'm always going to beat you at Chinese."

With his free hand, Adler smashed an imaginary pink ball on one imagined bounce against an imaginary wall. He whooped his exultation at the perfect shot and for having discovered the other's motive.

Kimmelman stopped shaking his head.

"Not revenge."

"Huh?"

"Not revenge. Let's just say I'm selling you a knish. I want you to buy, to have, to eat—a knish. Simple."

"I don't understand."

Supported by the palm of his hand, Adler leaned against the cart trying to puzzle it through. Maybe twice a year he and Kimmelman met for a couple of hours to chat, mostly about old times—who was in whose class, who did what to whom in the alley, pranks played on old man so and so. Last month they had gotten carried away—Kimmelman wasn't very good at drinking, let alone in bars—and had challenged him. But even in defeat, 21-6 at that, Kimmelman had been more exuberant than he, almost ecstatic. Maybe it wasn't revenge after all. What, then?

Suddenly, he was aware that his fingers were frozen. He looked down at the hand pressing upon the knish cart, then slid it rapidly over the top and down one side.

"Cold. Ice cold!" he shouted in accusation.

Adler flung open the oven door, pulled out the coal grate and the trays above, then rammed each back in turn. He slammed the door against the still protruding grate, shutting it noisily. He glared at Kimmelman.

"If you didn't want a knish, why should I make a knish? And if I didn't make a knish, why start the coals to heat what wasn't there?"

Adler stormed away. He'd been had and had badly. The delay had cost him several minutes as well.

"Potato or kashe?" Kimmelman called after him. "Artie!"

The name struck Adler between the shoulders.

"A choice must be made."

On a Sunday morning several weeks later, Adler snapped the rattan blinds of his living room window shut and strode along the corridor to the kitchen.

"He's here again," he announced in grim exasperation from the doorway.

"Hmm."

The woman did not look up from the Bloomingdale's supplement to the *Times*.

"I said he's here again."

"Who?"

"Kimmelman."

"What a bore."

She put the paper aside, and rising from the ice-cream parlor table for two, glided barefoot across the terra cotta floor to the cooking island. Bent forward, her head seemed lost amid the copper and brass that hung unsullied above her. She took a sliver of ersatz quiche (skim milk, lo-fat cheese, and egg substitute) from the warming tray and reached beneath the counter for a protein bar.

"How can he expect you, anyone, to eat that—that—?"

"Knish."

"That thing. What's it called?"

"A knish."

"Kintsh. You said it's not like . . ." she pointed to her plate.

"Hardly. I told you—it's a patty covered with dough and in Kimmelman's case filled with either mashed potato or ka—buckwheat. Both with onions. No matter what the filling, there's always onions."

She curled her lip in disgust and piled the quiche onto the protein bar.

"This would really make a marvelous hors d'oeuvre."

"Yes, they use them for hors d'oeuvres."

"Do they? And here I thought I had created a culinary masterpiece."

"What, the knish?"

"Kintsh?"

"Yes, the cocktail knish. Hors d'oeuvres, damn it!"

"This . . . this kintsh has certainly become a fixation with you, Arthur."

She reseated herself.

"Fixation? Fixation? Kimmelman's out there three times a week for God's sake. But what I want to know is not why—to hell with why—Nan, but why me?"

He had joined her at the table and held her by the wrist with one hand while pounding the surface with the other.

"Why me? Jealousy? Envy? Spite? Is it my fault that I've made it and he hasn't? That he's a city employee? That for him an apartment in Queens is the end of the line? But maybe that's not it either."

He released her, rose, thrust his hands into the shallow pockets of his jeans, and circled the island.

"After all, there are others from the old gang who've made it. There's Davey Slatkin the civil liberties lawyer—always in the papers and on the faculty of Yale Law. Okay, he's too far away. Even Kimmelman wouldn't drag himself and his gear to New Haven. But Mel Chernoff's right here in town with a practice in the Village and running a free clinic in East Harlem. And so is Ed Jacoby, head of EJ Enterprises, living on Fifth Avenue and on the board every organization from Friends of the Hudson to the UJA.

"I'm not even the biggest—yet. And I'm not such a bad guy either, Nan. Did I swipe his roller skates, cheat at cards, bloody his nose years ago? Who didn't? Kimmelman himself was no angel. And just two months ago, before all this started, I stood the drinks and picked up the tab for dinner. So, I ask you, why me?"

"Why me?"

"Why me?"

"Why me, Arthur?"

"What do you mean, 'Why me, Arthur'?"

"Why are you asking me? Ask Kimmelman."

Adler snorted.

"You haven't talked with Kimmelman lately. He sounds like the Delphic Oracle. Like my old Hebrew School teacher explaining the Bible. You think you understand, but when you unwrap the mystery of the language, you find there's nothing in the package."

"But Arthur, isn't an answer you don't understand better than no answer at all?

"Now you're doing it," Adler half-bristled. "But, okay—okay. I'll give it a try."

"The—the—what do you call it?"

"No. No. I'll ask Kimmelman."

"Good idea."

She rose, put her empty plate on the counter, and turned to embrace Adler.

"Hurry back."

She kissed him.

"And bundle up. It's cold."

"Oh, that's good. And you sitting here like a scene from some actual Naked Lunch."

"Brunch."

She kissed him again.

"By the way," he said, "the 'what do you call it'? It's also used to describe this."

He grabbed at her crotch and left her laughing as he returned along the hallway.

"Is it really? Kintsh? Is that like . . .? Nah."

She examined herself casually.

"With mashed potatoes—and onions?"

The front door slammed.

"Arthur, you're getting kinky as hell. Love it."

Adler huddled before the cart, arms folded, hands tucked into his armpits, his ski sweater all but useless at thirty degrees.

"All right, Harv," he insisted through chattering teeth. "I want to know. Why, me, huh? Why me?"

"It's your . . . " Kimmelman paused, reaching for the precise word, ". . . karma."

"Karma? Karma? A knish cart and karma?"

He folded his arms, momentarily flung open, once again bracing against the cold.

"All right, destiny."

"What destiny? When destiny? How destiny?"

"You are, after all, Artie, one of the chosen people."

"By you! Chosen by you! A madman. Do I have to prove it? Look. You've raised the price to a dime and still not a knish in sight."

"Overhead," Kimmelman lamented.

"Overhead? What—salt?"

Adler picked up the metal canister and dashed it against the top of the cart. He bent over, staring at the white spill.

"Real salt for fictitious knishes," he mumbled in disbelief. His face was close to Kimmelman's.

"Why me, Harv?" he pleaded again.

"Artie, not to worry."

He patted Adler's arm.

"Believe me, I'm a friend."

With his other hand, Kimmelman took a pinch of salt and tossed over Adler's shoulder.

"Good afternoon, Mr. Adler. Knish, Mr. Adler?

Engrossed in conversation as he was and because the cart had for months been so regular a part of the landscape, Adler had not realized it was there. He blanched and stammered.

"Harv? You here—today? It's Tuesday, Harv. You're not here on Tuesday."

"Extended hours. Better service. Knish, Mr. Adler?"

Kimmelman turned toward the bewildered, half-questioning other. But Adler ushered his companion along.

"It's right this way, Mr. Weeks. The first house."

As they walked on and up the flight of steps, bits of Adler's speech, like confetti, gusted back toward Kimmelman on the raw wind.

"Vendor . . . familiarity. . . are limits . . . old world delicacy . . . fillings (laughter) . . . exactly haute cuisine . . . have . . . de veau . . . ty nine . . . rare vintage . . ."

"Weeks," Kimmelman mused. He considered the near translucent pallor and wisps of surviving straw amid abundant gray.

"Definitely not."

Deft and decisive, he hung his tongs on the handhold.

"I've had it, Harv," an enraged Adler greeted him the next morning. "I've had it. You might have damn well cost me a promotion."

Kimmelman was concerned but unabashed.

"I hope not. I mean, I'd be the first to congratulate you as senior vice-president. But I'm no fool, Artie. I know bringing the boss home to dinner. It was all respect. It was 'Mr. Adler'. Believe me, I know my place."

"Well, your place isn't my place. Not anymore. I want you out—gone."

"Artie, Artie, I have my obligations too."

"You can oblige me by leaving. If not, I'll leave it to the cops and the courts."

"Also rights."

Kimmelman removed one of the price placards—now marked 20¢— to reveal his municipal license.

Adler sagged.

"At best, Harv, at best, you were—are—an embarrassment."

"Embarrassment. What is embarrassment? The misperceived failure of fact to conform to circumstance. But fact you can't change. Circumstance, maybe. If not, then all history—five years ago, five thousand years ago, five minutes even, is an embarrassment to those who have lived or received it."

"Harv, please. It's too early in the morning," Adler waved him off.

"Not feeling so hot, Artie? In a sense, French food is only for the French stomach. An acquired taste is not an adaptation. It's like Weismann and his mouse tails."

"Harv, you talk nonsense. Besides it was nouvelle cuisine."

"Not—not margarine, Artie!"

"Never! Butter—less, but still butter."

"For a minute you shook my faith."

"Spare the sarcasm."

"I am sincerity itself. Remember, Artie, it's welfare I'm into."

Adler looked at him hard. He couldn't tell. Either Kimmelman meant what he said or had convinced himself that he did.

"It was the wine," he confessed.

"Too much?

"Yes, in the pâté."

Kimmelman considered.

"A liver knish lacks authenticity," he remarked obliquely, restoring the placard to its holder.

Adler propped himself against the cart. But in an instant he sprang back with a cry of pain.

"My God, you've got the charcoal fire going."

Kimmelman bowed with a touch of proprietary pride.

"You're a puzzle all right, Harv," Adler went on, shaking his hands as he spoke.

"All winter you sit freezing your ass on the milk box, but now that spring is on the way you fire the damn thing up."

"As they say, for everything there is a season. I detect a warming trend, so . . ."

"There's no season for cheap word play or for . . ."

"My apologies—for that."

Unthinking, Adler reached forward once again. Fencer swift, Kimmelman drew his tongs from the handhold and with a single motion lunged toward Adler's errant hand, grasping it before it could touch the burning surface once more.

"Artie," he said, "I'm nothing if not into welfare. I'm telling you."

Adler reluctantly followed his guest out of the doorway into the glare of a late spring sun, half-hearing the lecture.

"Look, we're not talking one ward. We're talking a whole district. Not just your little upper middle class artsy-fartsy neighborhood here, but blue collars—Eyetalians, blacks and PRs in the projects and slums. Along the avenue you even got A-rabs for Chrisake. You got no chance in the primary if you don't hit the streets. Yuppies come lately or not, they mostly don't know from cocktail parties in Red Hook or Fort Greene. You gotta get out and meet 'em, shake 'em by the hand, stuff your face with ribs, goddam scungilli if you have to. Even this shit," the speaker gestured toward Kimmelman's cart as they approached, "for those two or three old time Jew votes."

"It's just not my style, Mr. Conroy," Adler stated, less in protest than in pride.

"What the hell are you talking about? Do you want a shot in the f"'n' primary or not? Here, I'll show ya. Let me have one o' them things. There's your halfa buck."

Kimmelman shook his head.

"Out."

"Out?"

"Out."

"He's always out," a sullen Adler explained.

"Always out? What the hell are you doin' here then?"

"At the moment I am providing free advertising space to my old friend's campaign."

Kimmelman patted one of the bumper stickers affixed neatly to the cart. 'Arthur Adler Assembly'. The bold blue caps with oversized initial A's stood out in sharp contrast against their white background.

"Nice colors, Artie; I forgot to mention."

"You know this guy?" a wary Conroy asked his charge.

"For years."

"Forever, Artie. Forever."

"You know this guy who never has nothing to sell? Or up here neither?" Conroy tapped his head.

"Even if I had, I couldn't sell to you," Kimmelman smiled.

"What d'ya mean?"

"Restricted."

"Restricted? Now hold on here just a goddam minute. This is America, buddy, and I'm a vet . . ."

"I mean," Kimmelman added, with a nod toward diplomacy, "I have only one customer. And even he doesn't buy."

Conroy stared like a baffled bulldog at an empty hole where a bone should have been.

"Let me get this straight. You sell this crap you don't even have to one customer who don't even buy:"

"Correct."

Conroy turned to Adler. "And you're friends with this guy?"

The would-be candidate squirmed between denial and affirmation.

"You're a regular piece of work, Adler."

Conroy backed away, shaking a thick forefinger in his retreat. "It's too late to withdraw, but I'm sure as hell not layin' out any street money."

Adler turned to Kimmelman. "Satisfied?"

"What are you worried about? It was a very long shot and you don't need the aggravation. As for him," Kimmelman tossed his head in the direction of Conroy's departure, "think about those old upstate pols going to a kosher deli to eat a 'saleahmi' sandwich or 'filtered' fish? Do you want that? Do you want to break your tongue on the double 'l' in 'pollo,' eh gringo? Or pronounce every letter in 'chitterlings' with flawless ofay diction? Don't pander. Don't pretend." Besides, you're doing pretty well at your present job, and any aggravation there is at least familiar.

"By the way, Artie," Kimmelman went on in softer tones, "the . . . lady. She's nice. Says hello every morning. 'Hi, Mr. Kintshman.'" For heaven's sake, Artie, you could at least teach her."

"I—I've tried," Adler apologized, head bowed and shoulders sagging. Sweating in the heat of the cart, the sun, and the conversation, he took a napkin from Kimmelman's dispenser and wiped his face and neck.

"Wait a minute. Wait a minute. What's this?" Adler's voice rang with agitation.

"That's authentic," he declared, pointing to a pile of irregular squares of wax paper weighted down with a brick. "But this— never. They never had napkins. Never."

"No," Kimmelman agreed. "But why such a purist, so absolute? Don't lay a nostalgia trip on me. Adjustments must be made for time and place. I never denied it.

"Take my uncle. He grew up in a shul where the old men gabbed, joked, passed snuff boxes back and forth, and hand painted signs asked you not to spit on the floor. Today, he goes to temple. The rabbi announces the page, the congregation listens to the cantor, and ushers seat latecomers or not depending upon which prayer is being said. Order and decorum. What has changed? My uncle? Yes. The packaging? Yes. But the goods, the genuine article, is the same.

"So, for you, Artie, I not only have preferred customer status—but a napkin as well."

Adler folded the napkin and slipped it into his pocket.

"Harv, I have a deal for you. You're here, what, five days a week?

"Six."

"Six?"

"Starting tomorrow, I'll just take Saturdays. After all, I'm only human. Everyone needs at least a day."

"Okay. Okay. Six days a week, then, you stand here trying to get me to buy one lousy knish that you don't even have for sale. Suppose I get you some real trade. There are always parties down here, at the office sometimes. Take your . . . wagon, let me alone, and I'll swing things your way."

"Artie, how long have I been here?"

"Six—eight months," Adler rasped.

"Then you should know I don't cater."

In desperation admitting no despair, Adler tried again.

"Well, how about this? You pick a site, anywhere—King's Highway, Fulton Street, one of the malls, Montague—not

Montague—yes, even Montague—and I'll set up a stand for you. Fixtures, equipment, help. You owe me nothing till you start turning a profit.

"Six—eight months. How many times must I say it, Artie? How many ways?" Kimmelman smiled and shook his head. "I'm not in the knish business."

Whether it was midsummer and its madness, the heat, that they were out of macadamias with half a pitcher of Manhattans to go, that he had drunk most of the other half, sheer hunger, or a concoction of all these (not to forget a dash of bitters), Adler slammed his copy of the *Voice* against the *Journal* on the ground beside the chaise and leaving the papers rustling in their mutual discomfort marched besandalled from the privacy of his enclosed garden, through the house, and out to encounter the omnipresent Kimmelman once more.

"How much is a knish?" he demanded through teeth all but clenched.

"One dollar."

"Well?"

"Well?"

"Well, where is it?" Adler challenged.

Kimmelman pouted in disapproval.

'That's not how you order. You don't just order a knish—an abstraction. It's 'May I have a camembert knish' or 'I would like a knish with tofu filling.' Be specific."

"All right. All right," Adler slammed a handful of coins against the top of the cart. "I'll take a buckwh—kashe, a kashe knish."

Kimmelman shook his head as he pocketed four of the quarters.

"What? No kashe?"

Kimmelman nodded.

"What've you got?"

"Name it." He slid the excess change toward Adler.

"Gimme a potato."

Adler's voice was tense, tight, almost shrill.

"Now you're talking. When everything is said and done, Artie, there's really only one choice."

Kimmelman lifted the tongs, opened the oven door and, gripping a tray with his apron-covered hand, slid it forward. Adler strained to see, eyes flashing in triumph at the bluff he had called. Then the tongs snapped at the rear of the tray, Kimmelman whipped a sheet of wax paper from the pile beneath the brick, and the knish lay steaming before him.

"Is it fresh?" Adler whispered.

"To your order."

Adler's head spun. His legs turned to rubber.

"Here, here," Kimmelman closed the oven door, grabbed Adler's arm, and kicked the milk box under him as he collapsed.

"I'm all right," Adler protested.

"Wear this. It'll keep off the sun."

Kimmelman removed his cap and placed it on Adler's submissive head.

Adler shivered.

"Chills and even sitting next to the wagon. This will help block drafts."

Kimmelman undid his apron, looped it over Adler's head, and draped it across his lap. Almost instinctively, Adler reached behind, tying a loose bow that dropped below his waist and obscured the brand name emblazoned above his rear pocket. With every heartbeat, the lurking figure on the breast of his shirt peered from behind the bib.

The trembling continued. Kimmelman removed his ragged coat and laid it across Adler's knees. Then, as if by force of weight, the shuddering stopped.

"Eat, you'll feel better," Kimmelman advised.

Adler sprinkled some salt over the knish then raised it to his lips and bit in.

"Good, very good," he said in full-mouthed staccato.

"A small lump or two, a black speck—burnt onion maybe, a little greasy—the real thing."

He took the knish with steadying hands and ravened the remainder, growing vigorous in his enthusiasm as he ate.

"Wonderful. I don't know how you did it, Harv. The taste," he licked his fingers, "the smell, just like on Pitkin Avenue."

Kimmelman smiled, indulgent.

"Just like on Hester Street."

"You've never been on Hester Street."

"Just like in Warsaw or Minsk or Kiev."

"You've got some nose."

Adler crumpled the waxed paper.

"Got any more?"

"Please," Kimmelman reproved.

"Sorry."

"Listen, Artie," Kimmelman confided as he bent above him. "You're not on Pitkin Avenue, and it's not like on Pitkin Avenue. Instant mashed. Yes. And what's the use trying to recreate Pitkin Avenue or what it was like? The tongs, the trays—all Teflon. After all, Artie, there was a Pitkin Avenue and you were on Pitkin Avenue and ate the knishes there. Who can say no? Who can take that away? Who can even make the attempt? Who, Artie Adler, but yourself?"

Kimmelman laid a reassuring hand on Adler's shoulder.

"By the way, there are more."

Adler opened the oven and drew out first the empty top tray, then the middle one, filled with potato knishes, then the third.

"Kashe!"

"I took a liberty," Kimmelman confessed. "A small joke, a reward for all these months of labor."

He turned to go.

Adler was not amused.

"Some things you don't fool around with, Harv. Kashe and potato is heavy stuff. We have our fun here in the Heights, but serious is serious."

Kimmelman rounded the corner and disappeared.

Adler groped about in his apron pockets and withdrew a stub of black crayon. One by one, he removed the price placards and carefully changed them to $1.95.

Sabbath Songs

Earlier, the wind gusting off Superior had blown the falling snow in great swirls. But now it descended softly, a curtain of ever-changing hexagonal beads hung before the hotel window, which together with the steady fall of evening blurred the view. Along the lakefront, ships and silos hulked indefinite through the graying mist, already ghostly constructs of the mind's art.

Howard Pereles gazed vacantly through it all, soothed by the steady quiet of the scene. Minutes ago, he had gathered the random litter of notes, memos, and drafts into neat piles and placed the final version of the contract in the attaché case that still lay open on the desk beside him. Then, loosening his tie and slumped in his swivel chair, he had turned toward the window seeking a moment's ease.

He had earned that much at least. His week in Duluth had been strenuous, unpleasant at times. Hours were long, bargaining difficult, and he was more than a thousand miles from home. Into a second decade as Vice-President for Sales, Pereles was no longer used to direct negotiation. But with the important North Central Industries agreement in jeopardy, he had had to step in. It was his now, save for the signing before tomorrow's flight, and no doubt Pennsylvania Machine and Tool would applaud him mightily on his return. But in his present enervation neither success nor applause seemed reward enough.

It was not a matter of simple exhaustion, nor of boredom, nor a reaction to the place itself. He had known this malaise at other times, in livelier cities, after only the second or third night in town. But the steady drab of Duluth in February, the stark geometries of its structures, the Gordian tangle of blackened wire and pipe in its Oz of industrial complexities, seemed to mirror his own interior landscape.

It was not loneliness either. He had Skyped once or twice, had telephoned liberally, and besides, Valerie, his sons, and the grandkids were somehow always with him, as if familial ties were infinite tethers or mooring ropes whose connection survived all distance. No, it was some other nameless attachment that he seemed to miss. Still, he was a domestic sort, and after a strenuous week it would have felt good this Friday evening to sit, brandy in hand, slippered before his own fire.

Now the street lamps were lit, their rays filtering through the snowflakes and beamed through two refractive flaws in the windowpane to dance diffuse and flamelike beside the attaché. Upon the desktop, blurred faces of his grandchildren and of their fathers as children themselves smiled through the pooling flicker of light. While wisping above them, as if through candle smoke, hovered Valerie herself, auburn and freckling in the glow, small mouth morphing toward smile, hazel eyes in chameleoned laughter. He called to her, but the music heard as he moved his lips was of a voice and language not his own:

"Lekho dodi likras kalo [Come, my beloved, to meet the bride] . . ."

Dressed in black hat and long black coat, a small man swayed from side to side as he prayed before the eastern wall of the room. Pereles recognized his grandfather.

Tsvi Hirsh Perelstein turned at once but gazed beyond his grandson to where Valerie still loomed above the desk.

"A zelkhe Shekhine hob ikh keyn mol nit gezen [I have never seen this sort of divine presence]," the old man said matter-of-factly. Then, turning back, he resumed his prayer.

"P'ney shabos nekabelo [Let us welcome the Sabbath]."

Once, without breaking rhythm, he glanced back toward the desk and shook his head.

Almost at his grandfather's behest, it seemed to him, a bride-like figure had appeared in the doorway. A crown of white lace woven through her hair matched the full-skirted formal dress that belled five inches above the double-hearted ankle bracelet, six above her white patent pumps. She moved unsteadily upon these and reached for a chair to balance herself, careful to use her right hand lest she crush the orchid wrist corsage on the left.

"Na—Nadine Novick," Pereles murmured. "Harrison Senior Prom."

She smiled in recognition, raising her skirt high enough to reveal the lipstick faces painted on her knees, also smiling.

"Knees are ugly," she shrugged, and slowly, slowly, bared her thighs.

For a moment, Pereles was spared the embarrassment of memory. His grandfather, lifting his eyes from the prayer book, strode scandalized up the aisle between the bed and dresser.

"Nafke [Strumpet]!" he shouted, flailing his arms so that the great wool talis nearly slipped from his shoulders.

She passed from his sight between pews. Tsvi Hirsh subsided and renewed his chant. Nadine drifted, skirt still high, toward Pereles, who now grinned and flushed remembering.

He had been very pleasantly surprised. Her parents, after all, were observant. No picking their daughter up for a Saturday date till after sundown. He saw them now—the father scholar sallow, the mother without wig though with hair that resembled one. But

Nadine—a good Jewish girl no doubt—yet somehow apart—from them at least—at least that night in June.

It hadn't taken much. Two kisses in the doorway—safe enough—the Novicks lived in the rear of the building—a touch above the waist—a touch below—then swiftly through the courtyard, led down tunneling cellar steps. He had seldom dated her before and till now, had not seen her since the summer after graduation.

Her smile and inviting portal of her thighs riveted him still.

"They'll turn blue with cold," he thought he thought, almost heard himself—heard someone—say it.

Another worshipper had entered. Lean, almost cadaverous, he paused in the doorway, glancing without turning his head from Perelstein in vigorous prayer to Nadine, who, if anything, stood with skirts raised higher still.

"A mass of contradictions, these Jews," he observed aloud with amused and casual detachment.

Nadine turned from Pereles at the sound. Her smile broadened.

"Wait, Nadine," Pereles pleaded, his voice edged thin with jealousy. "Stay with me. You don't even know him. That's Sherwood Miller. After your time—our time."

She seemed not to hear him. He let her go and tried another tack.

"Hey, Woody, how long's it been since the last reunion? Twenty years? Twenty-five?"

His old college roommate did not respond.

Pereles remembered that aloof pose well. Perhaps it came half of being the perpetual outcast, half of being a wealthy man's son. In Swannsburgh, both Jews and cash were scarce. Removed from his peddler great-grandfather by two generations of prosperous lawyers, but barred by acquisition and ancestry from the essential life of the town, Miller survived through disdain and self-derision. Whether, as a brash pledge, he mockingly assigned tasks to fraternity brothers whose fellowship he never made, or recited the blessing over bread as he munched an English muffin at services on Yom Kippur morning, his acts were of a piece—perverse, deliberate, disengaged. Sherwood Miller. A life in limbo. Uncertain of what heaven was or hell. Sure he wanted neither.

Nadine had reached him by now. But in passing she had once again caught the old man's eye. Her skirt now more modestly in place, he was less irate than before but shook his head severely at her bare arms and pointed alternately to the cashmere sweater over one of them and above to where the women's gallery should have been.

Having made no impression on Miller, she half obeyed Tsvi Hirsh, drifting apout toward the ceiling fixture. Perelstein returned to his reading desk before the closet door.

He had not quite reached it, when a slight, tanned, athletic-looking man entered, excused himself as he eased past Miller, and smoothing his dark tie and pinstriped suit, took a seat.

The rustle distracted Tsvi Hirsh. He turned, saw the prominent dome of the newcomer's bald head, then tugged repeatedly at the brim of his hat. The man smiled in comprehension, and reaching back into a battered Horowitz-Margareten Coffee carton, withdrew a clear plastic skullcap whose rim was marked in small, open block, pale gray letters, as if embroidered: "Hebrew Headdress Courtesy of Bryn Owen R. T." Perelstein might have objected to this naked ruse, but he had resumed his devotions the moment his signal had been understood. It was Pereles who turned, jarred by the movement from staring after Nadine.

"Carr? Carr in Zeyde's shul? With a yarmulke? Even that compromise of a yarmulke?"

The figure seemed to grin toward him, delighting in his disbelief.

He had known J. Ellis Carrington (formerly Jacob Elias

Kolodner) casually, for the most part, but over time well enough. A good tennis player in his prime, more than a match for him, and a member of long standing in the Bryn Owen Racquet Club. A member of the Bryn Owen Reform Temple slightly longer, and, more anciently, one of the first two men of the persuasion admitted to the house of Harley, Hanes, and Goode. Married to the former Phyllis Marsh. Two children—J. Ellis, Jr. and Meredith Marsh Carrington—both now with children of their own.

The thing about Carr, Pereles thought, was that he fit in—even here, even with that skullcap. Maybe, especially with that, as it created the illusion of compliance. He was nothing if not correct. Woody would hate him.

Besides, with Bryn Owen less than an hour from the city, Carrington might easily commute between two worlds without rejecting either. If he kept his heritage at arm's length, it was still within reach. Though his temple affiliation was more a matter of convenience than faith, he maintained some forms of religious practice, but well within locally accepted limits of propriety and taste.

Pereles recalled the Sabbath dinner ages ago to which an unwitting Carr had invited him. Valerie and the boys too. He saw them now in the tapering flame and pale smoke of the slender candles. Wine. Both reds and whites. Very dry, well-aged, and impressive—as were the bisque, the Stroganoff, the mousse and the slim cigars that followed. Only the braided loaf seemed ordinary and out of place. Later, knowing Carr better, he had joked about it.

"It was all first rate, Carr, but somehow it didn't grab my Unitarian soul."

Perhaps misjudging him.

"Whatever our diet, Howard," he had replied with some pique, "we Carringtons are Jews."

Much later, reconciled, in the locker room after Carr had defeated him in straight sets, they had confessed their original names.

"It had already gone from Perelstein to Perls. I just restored an e and added one."

"In the American market," Carr had observed, "packaging is all."

Howard's smile of recollection broadened as he watched the usually precise and fluid Carrington fumble with a prayer book—opening, closing, turning upside down.

"Backwards, Carr. It's in Hebrew. Opens right to left. A mass of contradictions these Jews," he crowed, winking toward Woody Miller.

But Miller had turned away, distracted by a commotion in the corridor. Ever increasing and nearly drowning out Howard's laughter, it now spilled into the room itself.

Israel Brenner, landlord of Howard's childhood, brim of his gray fedora turned up, barreled his bullock body up the aisle toward a front pew, his by dint of donation and the status of comparative wealth. Rosie Fromchuck, neighbor, was in close pursuit, closing the small gap with vituperation.

"The middle of winter you don't give heat? May you burn in hell! My kids are sick in bed. They'll die of pneumonia, it'll be on your head, may it be split open! It's freezing outside, no? An icicle should stab you in the heart. Look at him walking around with his jacket open. Maybe you're hot in the pants, too, you old buck you?"

"You cold?" Brenner growled. "Put on a sweater."

"A sweater? I'll give you a sweater. A woolen shroud I'll wrap you in. Let the moths and worms eat you together."

"You don't like it where you living? Move!"

"Move? May you be carried to the grave before your time. I'll move you. To court I'll move you. You know what the judge said last time. In jail you'll sit five days, freezing, your tokhes should fall off."

"Fe! What kind of talk? Look where you talking!"

"So where am I talking? For the shul you have money and for a few gallons oil not? For a donation you have money and not for putty, the draft shouldn't come in the windows? Sure, a hoo-hah you'll be here, while my kids are maybe dying. Reb Yisroel they'll call you, may you be in exile forever. To the Torah they'll call you. May you break both your legs on the way, and when you want to scream let your tongue be tied like a scroll!"

"Sha! The boiler they'll fixing Tuesday."

"Tuesday! We could die ten times over by Tuesday, may the blood freeze in your veins!"

"Wednesday, maybe."

"Daven, go daven. But I'm not through with you. Knock your jaws together—your false teeth should jump out and devour you. Let the name of God stick in your throat and choke you! Omeyn."

"'Meyn," Pereles muttered, his shudder and writhe easing as the fire and ice of argument resolved.

Rosie stalked off to the rear, thrust her ampleness into a back pew, and with arms folded across her chest, fingers drumming on her arms, she sat in toe-tapped waiting.

Close as the quarrel had been, Tsvi Hirsh had not looked back. The landlordic litany, long familiar, had blended with his own, in the America he knew almost an impetus to prayer. But Woody Miller had nodded his vigorous approval through it all, the scene confirming his theory of contradiction. J. Ellis Carrington had smiled, as if such raucous exchange still touched him, however removed from it he might now be. But, if anything, his bearing had become more formal, despite his change from business suit to tennis whites and Nadine now seated ornamentally beside him.

She had changed too. The skirt of her prom dress was gone, but, to the disappointment of Pereles, she had been wearing shorts beneath it. The lipstick faces on her knees had been altered as well, features rubbed out to leave the score 0-0 in earnest supplication.

"Valerie," Pereles murmured.

Eyes open a slit and familial faces in the flames once more, his wife's, still freckled, smiling above them all—ablur against the window—wavelets of light zagged in six-pointed star.

"Stain' glass, Stai' glass, stai' . . . Ahh," he lapsed.

A tapping. A slight, dark woman with close-cropped hair stood heels together atop a three-step ladder, tacking posters to the wall.

Tsvi Hirsh whirled at the sound and pointed a long finger in admonition.

"Keyn arbet oyf Shabes [No working on the Sabbath]."

The woman turned, stared at the old man with defiant eyes, then turned back and hit her final tack a resounding blow. She descended, stored her equipment in a corner of the room, and snapped the sleeves of her tweed suit into place. Tsvi Hirsh glared still; he did not like the type. But she had stopped, after all, and besides, whatever she had hung, he could just make out, was written in Hebrew letters. With a shrug and a sigh he went back to his holy book.

"Zeyde needs his lenses changed again," Pereles laughed to himself. "Those are the names of poets. Ar-nold, Bahy-ron, Tshuh-ser, Kol-ridge . . . ," he sounded them out slowly. "And . . . And . . . that must be Mrs. Scharf . . . from Harrison."

The woman came forward as he named her and seated herself close enough to the old man to hear his chant. She perceived, without feeling, the esthetics of it, but this daughter of a son of the enlightenment knew not a word of what he said. She recognized the tablets above the altar and guessed what the abbreviated inscriptions might mean. But the *shalt*s, derived from a world view incompatible with those of Darwin and Einstein and from a narrow tribalism incompatible with the teachings of Frazier and Freud, were unacceptable. Superficially, the *shalt not*s were respectable enough, but in their concern for property, and to the extent that property contributed to motives for murder, the hierarchical class structure of the society that produced the Decalogue was clear.

Pereles tuned out her thought. Anna Scharf's politics had never interested him very much. But those oaktag signs still fascinated. Keats and Yeats. Class after class he had marveled that they looked like rhymes but weren't. And only in transliteration, now, long decades after English 11, could he see the difference, ever so slight, as typographical fact: כיץ — ייץ.

"Keats—Yeats," he murmured.

Bored, unmoved by the old man's ritual, Anna Scharf reached for a book on the seat beside her. She opened it, stood, and faced the rear of the assembly.

"The problem of Raskolnikov," she began, "is the problem of contemporary civilization, but Dostoevski's solution, faith," she continued, turning to the final page, "is typical of the nineteenth century. Still, the economic basis of the crime and of Sonya's fate, especially as it shows the position of woman in a society that has not evolved to the point of proletarian revolution, is common to both that era and our own."

She paused, looked about the classroom, and continued.

"Nadine, in what way can Sonya's behavior be justified?"

"Who, me?"

Mrs. Scharf nodded, eyelids aflutter.

"Well . . ."

"Stand up, please."

Nadine rose, clutching Carrington's hand for comfort. His thumb stroked her thigh twice.

"I mean, she had to," Nadine stammered. "They were starving—her family. There was no other way. She couldn't help herself. It was freezing, and . . ."

"You're telling me," Rosie interjected. "A landlord like Brenner she must have had, may he swallow a live coal."

"Please, Rose, you must wait your turn."

"She knows her?" Pereles wondered.

"Turn?" Rosie bellowed. "His head I'll turn. Fat neck or no fat neck, I'll wring it like a chicken."

The chatter and roar behind him again drew Tsvi Hirsh from his prayers, and, looking back, he saw at once that three women were mingled among the men in the sanctuary. Astounded, he ran up the aisle shooing them toward the ceiling with indifferent success. Nadine ascended lightly, but Rosie shuffled about, while Mrs. Scharf stood rooted to her spot.

Undeterred, Tsvi Hirsh called to Brenner.

"Mekhitse [Partition]!"

Reaching into the closet, Brenner produced a collapsible dressing screen. Together, he and the old man raced up the aisle to separate the women from the men by entrapping them in one of the accordioned folds. Succeeding, they nodded in mutual congratulation and continued the service.

A pyrrhic victory. Rosie stalked behind the screen, grumbling as ever. Anna Scharf remained transfixed and adamant in exhortation upon Sonya's plight. Even Nadine, unable to resist Carrington, wafted herself down beside him, discreetly behind a fold, indiscreetly reaching through it for his hand.

"Had to," she whispered.

"He'll get from me yet," Rosie threatened.

". . . the people," Anna Scharf concluded.

Woody Miller, smirking as he pointed toward the scene, caught the eye of Howard Pereles.

"Woody, you know me!" Pereles called.

But Miller had turned away and did not look back.

"Shema Yisroel," Tsvi Hirsh sang.

Hear, O Israel . . . and, as if on cue, Malcolm Sperling entered. At the sight of his former Bryn Owen neighbor, Pereles moaned and turned his face to the far wall.

Though something less than Zion personified, Sperling had long and fervidly supported the Jewish state. Lately, however, he had flirted—cautiously and tentatively, to be sure—with qualified, partial sympathy for the American Friends of the Palestinian People. He was, after all, chair of the Learned Professions division of United Jewish Charities.

An Associate Professor of Integrative Social Science, Sperling now lived deliberately among gentiles—a sprinkling of blacks and Latinos included—as a matter of policy and academic faith. If, in private, his casual speech remained tinged with a contemptuous *goy* or pejorative *shvartse*, his political creed was still liberty and justice for all. He had been an early defender of women's rights, for instance, an advocate for ERA. His petitions and letters were composed with great vigor, and the writing often left its mark upon the issues of *Penthouse* bracing his longhand drafts.

Sperling, a house divided, took a seat. He opened his prayer book deftly to the proper page, and, joining Tsvi Hirsh's chant, was caught up in the rhythmic movement of the ancient body as well. Womb rock—recovery of primitive response—ethnicity—he computed. Sherwood Miller glanced at him, noting the blazer and crepe soled buckskins, then looked away, unaware that from his own point of view, to have known Sperling would have been to love him.

Pereles hated his guts. After all, a man must be more than a series of shifting propositions subject to revision according to the laws of boredom and current trend. Just as a face, he thought, must have features beyond the beard, bald spot, and opaque glasses he now saw.

"Who are you, Malcolm Sperling?" he demanded.

Sperling removed his glasses, behind which there were no eyes, and began.

"On the one hand . . . ," he paused, then turned from right to left and back, unable to decide which was the one and which the other.

Anna Scharf took his appearance as personal affront.

"Ridicule of physical defects is a most base form of humor," she admonished, eyelids fluttering so rapidly that only the whites could be seen.

"You'll doing this, maybe it wouldn't open up the eyes no more," a motherly Rosie advised. "By my worst enemy it should happen," she growled at Brenner.

Nadine rescued the moment. Without leaving Carrington's side, she stretched her nebulous arm across the room and with her ever-present lipstick drew eyes in the vacancies provided.

Perelstein was upon her instantly.

"Men shraybt nit oyf Shabes [No writing on the Sabbath]!"

"That's four times he's caught her," Pereles mused. "Maybe Zeyde has an eye for her too." The faint echo of a peddler's chant, heard betimes in childhood, wafted through the cavern of memory: "Treflikhe var'; zay nit keyn nar [First class goods; don't foolishly pass it up]."

As Nadine removed her hand from her bosom, lipstick once more secure, Tsvi Hirsh darted his eye about the assembly, and again, more slowly, back.

"Keyn minyen [No quorum of ten]!" he declared in dismay. "Es felt eyner [We're one short].

Contrary to his orthodox conviction, the old man had apparently included the women in his count. Sensing this as he continued in fervent motion, Sperling laughed in staccato triumph between syllables. His painted eyes crinkled.

"Der Toyre [the Torah]!" Tsvi Hirsh exclaimed, wheeling about and pointing to the closet ark. "Der Toyre. A tsenter [The Torah. A tenth].

Pereles dimly recalled the old custom of counting the scrolls as a tenth man to complete the required quorum.

"Khaim," Tsvi Hirsh called to him, gesturing toward the ark. "Khaim!"

"Vos, Zeyde [What, grandfather]?" he responded in a long disused tongue to his long disused Hebrew name.

For a moment he was as if snow blind. Then his eyelids closed once more, dropping him back into easeful dark.

"Zolst efnen dem oren koydesh [Open the holy ark]," his grandfather continued.

Pereles rose dutifully and with halting steps moved up the aisle. Behind the sliding doors were several scrolls held in place by wire hangers. He lifted one out.

"Loz zayn [Let it be]!" the old man ordered.

Pereles started. The scroll slipped from his hands and thudded to the floor.

A cry, as if of mortal pain, rose in chorus from the assembly.

"Darfst fertsik teg fasten," Tsvi Hirsh pronounced.

"You must fast forty days," the others echoed.

Sperling smiled at the double triumph of responsive recitation and bilingualism.

"Fertsik teg!" Pereles cried, recalling the prescribed penalty for this offense.

"Forty days," rang Tsvi Hirsh.

"Fertsik teg," the others chorused.

"Forty days! Forty days!" Pereles wailed himself awake.

It took him a long moment to see that in his fitful tossing he had knocked the contract papers from his open attaché and scattered them about the room. His head cleared.

"Scrolls!" he laughed to himself, then gathered the papers, and restoring them to neat order, this time closed the case. He looked out the window. No faces dancing in distorted beams. The snow had stopped. Duluth lay almost lovely in the clear night. The view reminded him of the Christmas cards still on the mantelpiece after two months—scenic but a little yellowed about the edges and slightly smudged.

Stomach rumbling, Pereles checked the time.

"Jesus."

He reached for the phone and dialed room service.

The Labors of Leonard Vogel

I have come after them and made repair
Where they have left not one stone on a stone . . .
—Robert Frost, "Mending Wall"

Putting on his overshoes and about to begin his working day, Leonard Vogel heard his wife call from the next room: "Lee, you have to be crazy to go out in such weather!"

"It's not so bad, Ev," he replied, "a little cold, a little wet. Besides, I'm local today, not shlepping to Queens or Staten Island." He paused reflectively then added sotto voce, "Snow would be another thing. I couldn't see the markers."

"So, go then," he heard her call again. "As usual, there's no stopping you. But bundle up."

Though hardly in response to her command, Vogel buttoned his fleece-lined raincoat over two sweaters up to the neck, pulled his black-leather cowboy hat (this item a rare indulgence) down to nearly his ears, fitted its drawstring to his chin to guard against the wind, then grabbed a leather briefcase with a well-gloved hand and set out.

He had been doing the work for years now. It seemed to him a far cry from running the tie shop. There, toward the last, his trade had not been very brisk, even before Father's Day and

Christmas. Casual Fridays had been increasingly followed by casual Mondays through Thursdays. And in the age of T-shirts and jeans, who needed ties? So he gave up the business and retired, the shop becoming first a gyro joint and, more recently, a vegan café.

His new occupation, obsession some would say, had come upon him gradually, a consequence of his random strolls through the grounds close to home and increasingly precise observation.

He ran an interior monologue as he walked. "Five or six blocks to the gates, maybe fifteen to twenty minutes, an hour or so inside, then another fifteen to twenty back. About an hour and a half altogether. If I get tired or too cold, I can always take a break in the office. They've known me there for years and will offer me a cup of tea or hot chocolate." Then again, aloud: "And the walking does me good—though that's beside the point."

The point, in great part, lay in the contents of the briefcase.

He had gathered the small stones himself, choosing the smoothest and, preferably, those with one flattish surface. These were gleanings from his own small backyard, public parks, patches of earth surrounding street trees and those dotting the pedestrian median along the Parkway. He could have, with fewer pains, purchased stones from any hardware store or garden supply shop, but the impersonality of purchase was not simply irrelevant to his purpose; it was antithetical.

Now, twenty yards or so inside the gates, he paused at the first cluster of graves. The site had prompted his work long ago, and he visited this section regularly, for sentimental reasons among those more pressing. The markers here dated from the second quarter of the last century to the first few years of the current one, with a single significant exception. More slender, darker, more tarnished by time than the rest was that of Oskar Lowenthal, d. 1883. For years, Vogel discovered, it had stood alone, but as spaces became increasingly scarce elsewhere on the grounds, Lowenthal's had been joined by its now surrounding neighbors.

Beyond the marker's physical appearance, what had caught Vogel's attention that first time was that Lowenthal's grave was the only one in the group that seemed not to have been visited. Unlike the neighboring sites, there was no traditional calling card of a small stone placed atop the marker or on the grave itself. Each of the others bore several stones, some a dozen or more, a few even several scores. "For him," Vogel had thought, "there is no one left to remember. Or, if left—maybe a great-great grandchild, but maybe also too distant—in miles as well as time." And then a sudden, inexplicable resolve: "So, Mr. Lowenthal still with the two dots above the "o", then I'll remember. Whatever it is—the birthday, your Hebrew name, the day you left us, that you were here for sixty-one years. Not very much, but enough. A person like all of us." And with that, he retreated briefly to the unpaved walkway then returned to place a stone on Lowenthal's memorial.

Afterwards, he had left one at each of his annual visits, or, in the early years, as needed, since the stones might be removed by high winds, torrential rains, or thieving hands intending them for use elsewhere. While those on other markers in the section were subjected to the same forces, their numbers and collective weight assured that many were left in place. And, as Vogel observed, in the vast majority of cases, those remaining were added to over time.

Today there was no special need to add to the stones on Lowenthal's marker. Those he had seen two weeks earlier on the anniversary of the first encounter, including the one he had placed then, were still there.

Bending before the wind and rain, he moved on, amazed still at how long it had taken him to realize that Lowenthal's case was hardly unique. Not until the second anniversary did it dawn on him that such abandoned dead were to be found throughout the cemetery and, as an all but certain corollary, in every other cemetery as well. By the third anniversary, he had devised a plan to address the problem. He would make regular pilgrimage to each of the cemeteries in the five boroughs and in the Long Island counties beyond Queens, acquainting himself with those denizens, who, like Lowenthal, had otherwise been neglected and apparently forgotten.

Depending on the age of the establishment, his visits might last a day or two, or more than a week. Having completed the work, he would return after a time to check for chance omissions. Such a check is what brought him out in today's foul weather, his briefcase (just one for follow-ups) filled in the event of oversights.

Apparently, he had been quite thorough two weeks before, having only to deal with four or five omissions before reaching the office.

From the start, the challenge of the work had not been weather or travel time and distance but the secrecy to which he had pledged himself almost unconsciously. This required subterfuge. To wit: he was doing genealogical research; he had taken up the hobby of collecting rubbings of unusual markers; he was studying the decline in familiarity with Hebrew or Yiddish given names as evidenced by variations among markers in family plots.

All of these explained the briefcases, housing a laptop computer, notebooks, and various art supplies—beneath all of which lay the stones. He went so far as to jot notes, compose observations online or download genealogical materials, and take two or three rubbings on most of his visits, sometimes sharing them with Mrs. Vogel. The two laughed together at such inscriptions as *Beloved husband, beloved father, beloved grandfather—all lies* and *What she went through, you shouldn't know from it.* But she would chide him if she noticed the stones:

"What's with the rocks? The rest of your gear isn't heavy enough?"

"Builds muscle," he might reply, "or at least maintains it."

"I see. A Charles Atlas of the senior set. Wouldn't it make more sense to work out with a few dumbbells and leave the rocks at home with the rest of the collection? And, by the way, how many hobbies does a man need?"

Still, Evelyn Vogel was a tolerant sort, even putting up with his overnights and extended stays at motels in places like Farmingdale where cemeteries were manifold and whose inhabitants vastly outnumbered the local citizenry.

"Call me eccentric," Vogel had said, "but I think I've earned the right to a little eccentricity."

She had agreed. They still had their shared time—movies, shows, vacations, dinners, falling asleep together on the couch while watching TV. And twice, preceding trips to New England and Quebec, she had accompanied him on one of his Long Island visits, amusing herself for a couple of days at the motel pool or a shopping mall while he worked and afterward ferrying together across the sound to Connecticut to begin what she considered their actual journey. He didn't gamble. He didn't drink. True, he had begun to chase women, but, she laughed as she recalled a rubbing, such a chase and such women "you shouldn't know from."

"Ah, Mr. Vogel," a cheery voice greeted him from behind a counter as he entered. "Not such a good day for those rubbings of yours, I'm afraid."

"How are you, Jeffrey? No, not such a good day."

"A cup of tea, Mr. V?" the woman seated at a desk facing Jeffrey's offered.

"That would be great."

"Two sugars, right?" she asked as she rose.

"Right, Karen."

She poured a cup for each of them, and the three chatted as they sat and sipped for ten minutes or so in the waiting area, interrupted only by a couple of phone calls. Small talk, nothing more about Vogel's business or theirs, except to note that it was a slow day with just a single burial scheduled after noon. Having drunk his tea and exhausted such topics as rain, rising prices, and reckless drivers, Vogel thanked them and then took his luggage and his leave, with all of them wishing better weather for his next visit.

"Nice people," Vogel thought as he headed back, bent still against the elements. "A little more of a relationship with them than with the others in the hinterlands. But this, of course, is home base for me. I'm here sometimes even when I'm not working."

He smiled at the last word, reflecting on whether it was appropriate to his spontaneous and apparently self-imposed labors. In all the years there had been nothing oppressive about his task. Yes, there were inconveniences—foul weather (today a case in point)—traffic jams—a cantankerous groundskeeper or two, but nothing negative concerning the essence of his commitment.

Still, there was something he found unsettling. Once or twice each year or two while placing stones, he seemed to see another figure similarly engaged—always at a distance, never clearly or completely revealed. He might perceive the back of a hand, a nose, a hat brim, a pant leg or hem of a skirt. And at times this would recur in another venue weeks or months later—for instance an April morning in Brooklyn then an August afternoon in farthest Queens. At such times his response was to turn away—almost instinctively. "After all," he told himself, "I can't do it all, and it's not like I have a monopoly." His unease lingered for a day or so then faded away. And until the next occurrence, he went blithely on.

And then as years passed, less blithely on as the weight and woes of age began to press more heavily upon him. At first, he shortened his work week from four days to three and later from three days to two, cutting out the follow-up visits in the process. "I'll catch them in the next cycle," he reasoned. Then the territories shrank, with the more remote parts of Queens and all that lay beyond abandoned. Toward the last, he was paying a weekly visit, weather permitting, only to the establishment nearest home. His sleep, erratic enough, was further troubled by thoughts of a succession that he could not possibly arrange.

In the twilight of his own fading sun, Leonard Vogel lay quietly in the hospital bed, eyes closed, Evelyn holding one hand. The others gathered round. "Who?" he seemed to ask, his breath raspy and shallow. "It's me, Dad," his son and daughter, recently flown in from disparate parts, whispered almost simultaneously. "Me, Gramps," his eldest grandchild added. Vogel rolled his head slowly from side to side, and with his free hand slapped feebly at the mattress. "Who? Who?" he seemed to say again, the sound now bubbling up with the dark secretion that stained his lips. If it was, in fact, a question, this time there was no answer. In any case, the man was now past hearing.

Just as Leonard Vogel breathed his last, Luisa Vidale bolted upright in her bed half a world away beaming with inexplicable revelation. Stepping swiftly across the small room, past a loom with its knotted tapestry in progress, she reached for one of several identical boxes on the upper of two shelves. Then, clutching the carton to her breast, she sat cross-legged on the thin carpet covering the splintered floor and opened it.

She ran her fingers through the small stones. Most of them were smooth, almost polished, having been retrieved from riverbanks, beaches, and the rims of tarns. Dressing quickly, she transferred the cache to a canvas tote bag and made her sandaled way along the dusty road toward the ancient burial ground.

Tokens of Esteem

Through the intermittent wintry mix of a gray December afternoon, Cantor Herbert Mittelman drove along the beltway toward Rochester. Though eager to reach his destination—it was, after all, his day—he drove slowly, mindful of the weather and speed limit as well as of the time to spare.

He was alone. Barbara, returning from a conference in Toronto, would meet him at Ealing Institute. David was driving in from Oberlin, stopping in Cleveland along the way to pick up Jordan. Deb had called yesterday from Milan; she would not be there.

He did not mind travelling alone. Such solitude gave him a chance to collect himself, to prepare—as if for Kol Nidre night or a concert—and, indeed, as guest of honor and recipient of the Kodaly Life Achievement Award, he was expected to perform. The Volvo was like a studio on wheels—quiet, spacious, private. He inserted a disc in the deck and ran some scales. Then he replaced it with another and, attending to the phrasing and pitch, listened to himself sing the three principal pieces and the three encores he had worked on for the past ten weeks. He shook his head once or twice in disapproval, muttering "Breathe! Breathe!" The final note of the second encore disturbed him.

"A little under there."

He listened to the third.

"B+," he said, evaluating the whole. "B+—A- — no, B+. Not too bad."

He seldom gave full approval—especially to himself—and was rarely more than half satisfied with a performance.

"Not too bad," he repeated, smiling this time.

It had been a stock expression of his father's. One of two possible replies to "How are you?" The other was "Not well." The old man had seen life as degrees of misery. Could he have heard his son this afternoon and thoroughly enjoyed the performance, he might have conferred the superlative—"at all"—" "Not too bad, at all."

His mother, well matched, had been similarly cheerless. He recalled her greeting the first time she had heard him perform professionally.

"The theater's so cold, Herbie. How come the theater's so cold?"

"I don't know, Ma. I thought they kept it at 72. So?"

"So? You always liked to sing, even when you were little. Come, it's freezing."

It seemed comical now at a distance of nearly thirty years and the space of two graves. "Death," as his father had said, "is the one sure cure for life."

But mindful now of past insensitivity, Mittelman recalled an instance of his own. As college students, he and Paul had attended a concert given by the pianist Firkusny. After the fourth encore, with the audience calling for a fifth, they had risen, shouting "No more! No more!" before collapsing under the weight of their own brash laughter and the artist's disbelieving stare. Firkusny played the briefest of etudes, bowed once to polite applause, then left the stage and did not return.

They talked or met still—he and Paul—once or twice a year. Having heard somehow, Paul had already emailed a congratulatory note. There was no reason for him to be here today. The Kodaly was hardly a Pulitzer or Nobel, and he had not attended when Paul received his prize from the Pacific Biochemistry Society. The paths between Rochester and Irvine seldom crossed, as cantor and chemist moved in distinct orbits about the working centers of their separate lives.

He thought of concentric ripples widening in a pool. Then the wind rose in squall, riveting ice bits to the glass. For a moment, Mittelman seemed encased in steel and crystal. But turning the defroster high and using his wipers and wash, he managed to clear the windshield. Then the wind diminished—decrescendo.

He checked the mirrors and glanced across the highway divide toward the oncoming traffic. The early December weather and the promise of sports on TV had kept volume light. They were less bulk traffic than individual cars—single, separate—sharing for a moment a stretch of road as they bore their passengers tight in their compartments—curve, lane change, and ramp—toward diverse destinies and destinations—home and Sunday dinner, the mall, adventure, work, the grave—for a predictable few, or Ealing and honor.

Mittelman himself had changed lanes—or at least stopped straddling them—long ago. In his senior year of college for the first time, choosing against medical or dental school and applying instead for three years of intense training at one of the smaller conservatories. Even if he had satisfied the pre-med/pre-dent requirements, what scientific bent, really, was a Comparative Literature major with a Theater minor likely to have had? And the lessons, first piano then voice, with some theory and composition to boot, had never stopped completely. At the moment of crisis, he knew that his life should be in music—whether at the opera, or on the bandstand, or in the next Broadway hit he did not know. His mind's eye had seen his name in lights, upon myriad programs; an id's ear had heard the applause, the bravos, the drum roll and cymbal crash of standing ovations.

Vague and unfocused as it was, he had chosen the dream. Somehow, he had withstood the loss of approval—parents', friends'—and his own self-doubt. His increasing, if modest, success—as a pop singer in some of the smaller, fading Catskill hotels, vocalist with the busier wedding bands, participation in two or three of the more prominent chorales—with an occasional solo—had helped. Later, there would be the indifference of the talent agents, the two opera competitions ending with his elimination in the first round, the realization.

It had been rather like the deep underpass he approached now—an open world of boundless possibility reduced to a narrow confine of limited vision. Mittelman turned on his headlights. There had been no such easy illumination then.

But there had been Ginzberg—lecturer in Jewish liturgical music, on leave from the cantorial college. He knew.

"Too much voice for the bandstand, Mittelman. Too much for the supper club. Besides, is that the music you want to sing? On the other hand, a Merrill . . ." he paused, shrugging and shaking his head, as if the honesty of gesture were less painful than spoken truth.

"Broadway? A possibility. It's rich, strong. But, tell me, what roles? You're no leading man, Mittelman. Could you be content to be a 'guy' among the 'dolls'—a second—what do you call it—fiddle?"

"Banana."

"Banana? Banana. And for how long?"

Perhaps not much longer than the long silence that followed.

"Tell me, Mittelman," Ginzberg said at last, "Do you go to the synagogue?"

"Sometimes."

"How often?"

"High holidays. Three or four times a year otherwise. Like everyone else."

"Not like everyone else. With everyone else there's no otherwise." He paused. "Do you believe?"

"In God?"

"In God. In Yidishkayt. In Erets Yisroel. Whatever."

"I . . . I'm not devout. I mean, I observe some things—holidays. I don't keep Shabes. I . . . don't keep kosher."

"Kosher. Shabes. All you New York Jews are the same. You think it's all the rules or nothing. Listen, my Aunt Tillie in Philadelphia goes to shul every week. She's active in Hadassah—vice-president of the sisterhood. But every day for lunch—on toast—it's a shrimp salad. Is she devout? Does she believe?"

"I eat shrimp salad."

"Mazl tov. That's not the point. There are 613 commandments. Do you think you could manage to keep—say—429 of them or 364—or—a bare majority? And don't forget there are some congregations that don't know from kosher and some that know from Shabes like at a wedding the husband of a second cousin knows from the bride or groom.

"Congregations? What are you talking about?"

"I am talking about cantors. Jobs are going begging. There are places in the college. I'm recruiting you, Mittelman."

"Now, wait a minute . . . I'm not religious. How can I get up there and . . ."

"Excuse me—excuse me. Two months ago I heard you sing in La Bohème. Marcello. Are you really a 'bohemian'? Do you really paint? Are you living in Paris—in an attic yet—and not three rooms in Brighton Beach?"

"But that was acting."

"Now, it is acting. Now, it is Mittelman who was acting Marcello. But then it was only Marcello. No Mittelman."

"A cantor is an actor?"

"A cantor is a representative—of all the possibilities, all the hopes, visions of the congregation. Of course, he is himself unworthy. Who isn't? Remember the Hineni prayer you studied: 'Behold me without good works . . . a suppliant for thy people Israel who have sent me . . . though I am unfit . . .' When you chant you are the messenger—not Mittelman. And the music itself—never mind the words—is a form of prayer. The Kh'sidim will tell you that— even they are right sometimes—and that faith in the usual sense might follow. On the practical side, a cantor could have time for his other musical interests—and I don't mean bar mitsve lessons. You could give concerts, join choirs—even secular, I mean—maybe lead one—compose if you have the gift."

Mittelman sat impassive, astonished, mute.

"Look, a minute ago I told you what or who you couldn't be. But, after all, there is only one thing you can be—Mittelman— with all his limitations and his few strengths," he half-jested, almost as if speaking of himself. "And becoming a cantor might just be the way to make the most of yourself. Maximum Mittelman. Really. Think about and let me know."

Ginzberg's talk had hardly convinced him, but it had opened him to a possibility he had not considered. It had provided, despite his many doubts, some welcome point of light—a mark of tunnel's end—which grew larger and more brilliant over time and from which, changing lanes once more, he had gradually emerged.

Fingers of cold mist had begun to grope their way in from Ontario. He hoped Barbara had not been delayed. Over the years they had often seen so little of each other in their daily lives that milestones like the Kodaly had taken on exceptional significance, as reminders of their bond and opportunities to reaffirm it. They had been rather like two interlocking rings, occasionally overlapping almost completely, more often touching at a single, stressed point, most often waxing and waning irregularly in the orbits of each other's lives.

It had been his education at first—the years at the cantorial college. She had supported them out of her junior high school teacher's salary, while he, catching a day of substitute teaching here and there, was in class, the library, or rehearsal at all hours, six days a week. Later, after Jordan was born, it had been her education—a degree in library science. And later still, after Deborah, another in public administration. To accommodate, Mittelman had juggled his schedules, missed a light opera society meeting or two, turned down a recital, Babysitters, briefly a nanny, had filled the remaining gaps.

Such arrangements had been difficult but not so destabilizing as the frequent moves. Two years in Tampa, two more in Denver, four in the Twin Cities or environs thereof. A merciful six in northern New Jersey, where towns lacked a major hub and were in good part bedroom communities of New York. Add to this the anxiety of a short-term contract, clashes with rabbis and congregation presidents, auditions, interviews, travel.

Barbara, meanwhile, had been pursuing her own careers, first as a librarian, then as a library administrator. It had been clear from the start that she would not be his appendage—the cantor's wife. It was she who had initiated the final move—to Rochester, having been offered a directorship of regional libraries.

It was now he who followed her. Though he had not been unhappy at B'nai Torah, then in the renewal year of his third contract—with excellent prospects for a long-term appointment, he had been growing stale, complacent, had been reduced appreciably to the status of another suburbanite with a decent job, to one of the faceless millions in the vortex of the great cosmopolis. In so compact a place as Rochester he might find himself again. Learning of a vacancy at Temple Etz Chaim, the second largest congregation in the region, he applied and was invited to audition. He sang. They offered. He came.

The fog thickened, enveloping him in a sudden rush and just as sudden blew by. For a moment the glint of pale sunlight shone at the edge of the horizon, then subsided to monochromatic gray once more.

It had been a good move. Rochester was a livable city despite its eternal winters. There were good restaurants, theater, much music. In addition to native talent, Ealing and the universities, local and regional, brought in performing artists, troupes, lecturers. With only slight effort, one could lead a more than decent cultural and intellectual life. And for enrichment, escape, or excitement, Toronto lay but a few hours north and west across Lake Ontario while to the south and east the Finger Lakes, with their gorges and vineyards, offered a retreat to nature.

He had prospered. Well respected at E. C. for his cantorial and teaching skills, he had been given a lifetime contract in his fifth year. He had founded the Genesee Art Song Guild, performed at concerts (fundraisers in the main), given recitals (some of them in Toronto), composed works for the synagogue and beyond—his oratorio "Moses at the Burning Bush" was still in progress—and one semester a year taught Jewish liturgical music at Ealing. He had more than fulfilled Ginzberg's prophecy. He had, as a teacher at least, in a sense become Ginzberg himself.

An old blue Chevy coupe sped past him, raucous muffler and engine audible even through the sound-seal barrier of his own vehicle. Mittelman looked after it.

No—couldn't be David. Wrong road, wrong direction. And driven much too fast. Not that David wouldn't speed. Stopped for doing 75 in a 55 zone just three weeks after getting his license. Two months without the car keys seemed to work. Besides, he's not the type to push the limits that far. Would never do 90.

He hadn't seen David since August. He missed him. It was not just that David was the last, with one wingtip still brushing the nest, but that he was the most accessible of the three—less volatile than Deborah, more purposeful and open than Jordan. Perhaps it was all biochemistry—he'd have to ask Paul next time they spoke—perhaps the stability of living in one place for so long and of having been born to parents who were secure in their careers and in themselves.

A junior now, majoring in fine arts, he seemed headed more toward graduate work in art history or museum conservation than toward his own studio and garret. But he would choose—neither sensibly nor impulsively—for, in his case, heart and head were most often at one.

A hitchhiker stood on the shoulder, obligatory thumb raised. His face bore no expression. His sign read "Anywhere."

Better than "nowhere." Now, that's a sign for Jordan. All right, so he's finally found something to do—cameraman. He can survive—even live, decently. And he likes the work. Always liked—phenomena—train derailments, meeting the oldest man in Minnesota, knowing the number of rivets in the George Washington Bridge. Facts without concepts, things—numerical, tangible—but clutching them—like—charms against feeling—protecting, concealing himself—almost—behind these barriers to connection.

Yes, he had friends—always had—at some level. But how many had seen his studio apartment littered—as at home—with magazines and clothes—his collections of handbills, ticket stubs, cork? And how many had entered that other, darker room?

Possibly the best mind of the three—in terms of raw intellect—but also the least disciplined. Thirty-two and still in bud. Who knows whether he will ever bloom—so who knows whether to hope—or mourn?

He took the next exit and cloverleafed onto the state highway. He slowed—perhaps suddenly reluctant as he approached his destination—like all initiates before the rite. But, again, the road had narrowed and the cityscape—almost barren of people, loomed a ghostly distraction. A billboard for Shively's caught his eye. It reminded him of one he had seen years ago of a holly-wreathed model in mink who advised in red and green letters, "This Season Make Her Yours Fur-ever."

Deb did better than that.

Working in Shively's advertising department for the summer between her sophomore and junior years at SUNY Purchase, she had turned out a billboard and newspaper ad that he remembered well. It had shown a group of scattered little red schoolhouses, all marked "Shively's," with child models clad in the latest fashions bracing the sole of one foot against them. The text was simply "Back to School."

That was her—the cleverness, the eye for design. Buying for Saks—ideal. Had chosen her own clothes before she could really talk. And her crayoning—paper and walls—was more often pattern than scrawl.

Yet, in the end, her art was just—a servant—of glamour—of the will to wealth. She lived—how—elegantly. Hollowly. Too young—the gods she worshiped. Novelty itself. Where were spirituality, the shaping of personal perception whether within or apart from tradition, significance? Too old—these gods—too enduring—a threat to all things—like changing styles—that do not last.

The high priestess of pizzazz. And her devotion had gotten her—literally—where she was today—Milan.

Well, the boys will be here at any rate. Haven't seen all of them together in three years—a couple of holidays aside. For my funeral they'll be there.

Mittelman snorted at this involuntary intrusion of self-pity and shook his head.

Pop's ideas and Mom's syntax. A deadly combination.

He remembered his father receiving a bottle of champagne and vowing not to open it until his own children were all present once again. When at long last it was opened, the cork, like his father, had shrunk and the wine spoiled.

Funeral. The last chance for status. Mom and Pop kept score: "There must've been sixty cars. Five hundred people at the chapel." Missed out on their own. Some dozens for him, fewer for her—without the union members and relatives who had died in between. Who will be at mine? How many? This afternoon might tell. After all—a life achievement award. Some finality in that.

But his own life had not been achieved; some of it—perhaps the core of it—never would be; yet he would work unceasingly—he knew that. Retirement, when it came, would mean less time at the temple, more in the classroom, studio, and study. Should he no longer be able to sing without embarrassing himself there was composing to be done—the cause of music to be fought for and funded.

He thought of Dave Singleman—not for the hundreds of salesmen and buyers at his fictive funeral but for still selling at eighty-four and dying the death of a salesman on his way to Boston. Like Singleman, unlike Willy Loman, at least—at most—he had his vocation; there would be that if there were nothing else.

At 1:45 he stood in the auditorium glancing about at the sparse assembly. Barbara had not yet arrived.

A large man approached, extending his hand in exuberant greeting.

"You're Hubert Mittelman, aren't you?"

"Herbert Mittelman. Yes."

"Herbert. . .right. Sorry. Dunstan Caldwell—recording secretary of the Music Education Association."

"Oh, yes. I believe I remember you from the annual meeting last spring."

"Did you attend that one? Splendid session, wasn't it? Now, I'm master of ceremonies today, so let me just fill you in on procedure."

He rested a beefy arm about Mittelman's shoulders, and gesturing with the other, walked him twice about the room.

'If that's clear, Hubert—Herbert—then I'll see you on the stage in ten minutes," he said at last and abandoned Mittelman at the rear of the house.

Some others had arrived. He recognized the concert master and principal bassoonist of the orchestra. Two elderly members of the synagogue choir, Harriet Gorelik and her sister Muriel, came up to greet him.

"What a wonderful honor, Cantor. We can't think of anyone who deserves it more," Harriet gushed for both.

'Thank you, and thanks for coming."

"Our pleasure," Muriel murmured as they drifted away.

He noticed the temple's custodian, Wister Ferguson, standing with his wife in a side aisle, and began walking toward them. But a loud, throaty "Herb!" from behind stopped him. He turned. It was Morton Goldhaber, Congregation Beth Hillel, Buffalo.

"Mort! Good to see you. Glad you could come."

"Well, how often do they honor a cantor?" Goldhaber asked as if in collegial commiseration. "Besides, the Bills don't have a Sunday game this week. Ross is here too. Also Immerglick. Mazl tov again. We'll catch up with you afterwards."

He had known Goldhaber for nearly fifteen years. The others almost as long. They had worked together on committees and symposia on such topics as "The Role of Music in Jewish Education" and "Congregations, Cantors, Conflicts." Goldhaber and Immerglick had introduced one or two of his small compositions into their services, while he and Ross had conducted a running, friendly debate about the status of the art song in the early twenty-first century. The three were an engaging trio—not quite musketeers—but far less competitive and professionally jealous than others he had known. Had he not been living at a distance of some three score and ten miles, he might have made a near D'Artagnan to their approximate Athos, Porthos, and Aramis.

Mittelman glanced at his watch, then made his way toward the stage, scanning the room for Barbara and his sons as he went. She was not to be seen, but as he approached the steps the young men entered. He hugged David, who kissed him on the cheek.

"Sorry we're late, Dad. I had a flat, then hit some snow squalls. And Jordan oversleeping didn't help."

Mittelman turned to his elder son and half-slapped, half-patted his face.

"Yeah, yeah. I shaved," Jordan responded to his father's surprised look. "I always shave on Sunday whether I need to or not."

He followed Mittelman's gaze.

"I'm breaking the suit in for a friend. The tie is Davey's. He carries a spare—maybe he should do the same for tires."

He shot a heavy fist at his brother's shoulder.

"And, yes, I changed my underwear. Sunday, again—like clockwork—lucky you."

Mittelman grinned and shook his head. Despite the disorder of his life, Jordan was likeable, even endearing at times—a cross between Unwashable Jones and Pigpen of the comic strips.

"What's on the agenda, Dad?" David broke in. "Stones' tunes, Springsteen, Pink Floyd?"

"The Beach Bums, New Yentas on the Block, and Ungrateful Wretches," Mittelman responded in kind.

"Classics all," Jordan observed.

Mittelman reached toward a stack of programs at the foot of the stage.

"Have one."

The younger men took them dutifully.

"And sit . . ."

"In the first five rows," Jordan began.

"So I can keep an eye on you," David completed the thought.

"Wherever you like," said Mittelman.

They laughed together. There would be no running up and down the aisles today, and flying paper airplanes was at least unlikely.

"I have to go."

Mittelman ascended the steps.

"Break a vocal cord," Jordan urged.

"Yeah, Dad, me too."

"And keep an eye out for your mother."

"Who?"

Mittelman dismissed Jordan with another playful tap on the cheek, and David put an elbow to this brother's ribs as they went to find their seats.

From his assigned place on stage, Mittelman looked out over the audience, counting the house as he did at services. Fewer of the maroon plush spaces seemed vacant now. The room held about three hundred. He guessed that about a hundred thirty were in attendance with two or three minutes to go before the formalities began. He did not know whether to be disappointed or pleased. Already there were proportionally more people present than on a typical Sabbath morning; still, this was rather a high-holiday event. He'd wait for latecomers and see.

He noticed his sons in the fifth row—old habits died hard no doubt. They waved—Jordan frantically with both hands. He nodded. Other faces emerged from the crowd as well. Dan Zelinka, the vice-president of Etz Chaim, was there, seated next to Marilyn Weil, the rabbi's wife. After a puzzled moment, he recalled that Weil himself had had the Teitelbaum funeral at one o'clock. Kurtz, his own third-year assistant, was with him. Perhaps they'd make it yet. Perhaps, also, Steve Teitelbaum's death had kept others away. A past president and member of the board of directors would surely have garnered friendships, a following, respect. Still, a quick scan of faces told him that the congregation was represented decently. He noticed Harriet Gorelik and her sister seated toward the rear and, in a cluster halfway between them and his sons, members of his Sunday morning cantillation class—seven or eight—Ed Pinsky, Marv and Julie Barish, Sarah Krupnik, Phyllis Hurwitz, the Edelsteins, one other, he thought, whom he could not make out.

He rose as a figure came toward him and took the proffered hand. It was Ealing's associate dean, school dignitary designate, who would be seated across the stage.

"Congratulations, Cantor Mittelman."

"Thank you very much, Dean Ebersole."

"I'll try to keep it short. My remarks," he said, responding to Mittelman's puzzled expression.

"Oh, take as much time as you need. It's your house, and you're the host."

Yes, but you are the man of the hour."

Mittelman smiled in unaffected appreciation.

"Thank you."

"My pleasure."

The dean receded. Mittelman sat once again and resumed his survey. There were the cantors from Buffalo together with a fourth. He strained to make him out.

Looks like Sklar, Rainer Sklar. It is. Well, this is a pleasant surprise. Haven't seen Sklar in nearly three years—since the last recital in Toronto. Some gray in the beard now. Gained some weight, too.

Mittelman stroked his own abundant abdomen as Dunstan Caldwell sat down beside him.

"We'll be starting momentarily."

"Fine. It's nearly five after as it is."

Caldwell said nothing but instead reviewed the scant notes on his two index cards.

Mittelman studied the audience once more. The cantorial quartet had turned to greet a tall, slim figure, slipping into a seat two rows behind them. This was a surprise of another sort. Elliot Ehrlich of the Greater Rochester Jewish Center, the rival cantor of the rival congregation. Not that there was any animosity, even strain. But their relationship had been purely professional. Ehrlich had come, he supposed, more out of courtesy than friendship and if politics entered at all, to avoid even the appearance of a snub.

At least the local cantors would be represented—even if it was by Ehrlich. Shreiber? Away at his nephew's wedding in Boston.

Gelfand? Leading a tour group in Israel. (He would have to pick this week.) And Yanovsky, long retired and hardly able to speak these days, much less sing, hospitalized once more.

Hospital. Must call Jerry this evening. A second heart attack in three years is no joke. First Uncle Nat. Pop. Now Jerry. Certainly looks like a pattern. I'll have the cholesterol checked—again. Maybe after the first of the year.

His brother, surely, would not be here today. Nor would Rochelle, his sister, called away to Pompano Beach weeks ago after the difficult birth of her granddaughter.

The more precarious the more precious—this life—especially so at outset or end.

Mittelman started, then rose to greet the slight figure that bent above him.

"Congratulations, Cantor."

"Thank you." He studied the woman before him. "Have we met?"

"I'm so sorry. I have the advantage of you. Ellen Ranieri, director of music education for the school district."

"Oh, yes, the guest speaker. I saw your name in the program. Congratulations on the new job. And thanks for the invitation to next month's meeting. It arrived in Friday's mail."

"I hope I can call upon you for suggestions from time to time."

"Feel free."

She smiled a farewell and retreated to join the associate dean.

"Any second now," Caldwell advised as Mittelman resumed his sweep of the auditorium.

No sign of Barbara. Head of the voice department though. Siegfried, Herron—a few other chamber players. Mazzoli and Kang among the pianists. A bit more than half full now.

Who were all these others? Association members probably. Friends and colleagues of Ranieri too.

He checked the program. There were a student pianist and a chamber quartet.

Their families, friends, and teachers besides. Well, why not? This was the Music Education Association of Western New York.

"Time," Caldwell said. He rose and took the rostrum.

Though Mittelman began by attending to Caldwell's remarks, his focus soon drifted to the audience, searching for Barbara but finding instead some other familiar face here or there. Comparing the irregular patterns of maroon spaces and filled seats, a conditioned reflex, he counted the house once more. It was a respectable turnout at least.

Occasional words and phrases of the speech in progress washed back to him—"education association"—"welcome"—"followed by a short program"—"Herbert Mittelman"—he started, then relaxed—"school district"—"our host today". . . He was startled again by polite applause as the associate dean rose to speak. He listened as far as "it is my pleasure" then relapsed.

The distance between the stage and front row loomed gulf-like before him. It always had—even in the smallest of rooms. Even in the cluttered lounge of Heller's Hideaway, where, standing on a four-by-four platform eight inches high, he could reach out and touch the audience. He never did. Sometimes—later—with the music perhaps— but then he had had some help—the atmosphere, the special occasion, the joy—or pain—or guilt of his listeners—working with him.

At root, it was a solitary thing this music—solitary in its study and practice—even teachers and accompanists too often reduced to tools toward perfection. And performance—at best—was paradoxical. Yes, they—so often, so many—faceless—could be heard, seen en masse, but with the stage as pedestal—even the paltry one at Heller's—human contact, beyond the musical moment—was impossible.

He imaged an isolate wolf calling from the edge of a desolate precipice.

The sound returned—was it echo or response? *Perhaps—to cry out one's presence—in the wilderness—is the best each of us can do.*

Mittelman continued his search. If anything, the gulf seemed wider now, perhaps treacherous.

Still no Barbara.

Applause. The dean had given way to Caldwell once again. Applause once more as Ellen Ranieri came to the microphone. The program listed her address as "Music Education: Prospects, Purse Strings, and Progress." Predictable enough, Mittelman thought. Prospects would be dim and progress slight unless more money were made available. An ancient litany, but presented now with both sincerity and vigor that resulted in bursts of spontaneous clapping and a final sustained ovation.

"Thank you. Thank you, Dr. Ranieri," Caldwell regained control as the sound subsided. "All of us in the Association will surely join with you in working toward the goals you have set today.

"And now, let us turn to the central event of the afternoon, the presentation of the Kodaly Life Achievement Award. It goes this year to a man outstanding both as a musician and as an educator, a man whose voice has grown familiar to you from the cantor's lectern at Temple Etz Haim, the recital halls here at Ealing and elsewhere on both sides of the Lake, a voice that in times past was heard also on the musical stage and in cabarets. But our honored recipient is more than a singer. He is a composer of art songs and liturgical music and a choral conductor as well. But he is more than a composer and conductor; he is a music educator par excellence and music's ambassador to the public at large. . ."

Who was this person so described? A line from Eliot surfaced in Mittelman's memory: "Fixed in a formulated phrase." Was this, in fact, he? An aggregate of concrete actions, palpable events? A mere chronicle filled with dates of tenure, lists of works completed or in progress, numbers in attendance? Where was the flesh? The blood? The texture and nuance? The life itself?

He could hear nothing of his anxiety before performing—the sweats, the diarrhea—the chill of composing at three A. M. on a January night because he had awakened restless with a theme humming through his brain—the swathing comfort of applause or the smiling agony of accepting it for a performance he felt ill done—the frustrations of dealing with committees and boards slow to accept innovation. Where was he—the other Herbert Mittelman—the more essential—perhaps—perhaps more—"

" . . . pleased to present the Kodaly Life Achievement Award to Cantor Herbert Mittelman," Caldwell concluded.

It was only the applause that spared Mittelman from the faux pas of obvious inattention. He strode to the rostrum, smiling, took the bronze plaque from Caldwell and shook his hand.

"Mr. Caldwell, Dean Ebersole, Dr. Ranieri, members of the Association, friends and guests *(speaking of formulated phrases)*."

He suppressed a smile.

"It is with both humility and pride that I accept his award—humility because my colleagues and peers, at least as worthy as I, have chosen to honor me—pride in that my few accomplishments have called themselves to such favorable attention. *(Where does grace end and groveling begin?)* This is a day of thanksgiving. In effect, I am being thanked by the Music Education Association of Western New York and by you who have gathered here for my small contribution to music and music education. I accept that thanks and offer my own for the honor and award.

"But I also must thank others who have helped make my career possible—my wife, Barbara *(who still has not arrived, I see)*, for her patience and interest, my children for at least attempting to understand why I missed some of those ball games and school pageants *(Why, Jordan, are you burying your face in your hands?)*, the members of Temple Etz Chaim for giving me the latitude to create both within the synagogue and without *(especially since Harris Wilner retired to Florida and Lou Bailin resigned from all committees)*, my mentor, the man who pointed out the path I have chosen and followed, the late Isaiah Ginzberg, and for what talents I have and the ability to use them *(you don't get the whole of me Ginzberg)* the power that infuses us all.

"But this honor is not simply personal. I stand here today as representative of the thousands of music educators everywhere *(play nice, Herbie—share the toys)*, whether in kindergarten classrooms or in conservatories. Their job, our job, is indispensable to the cultural and spiritual growth of young people and hence to the future of civilization itself. So, on their behalf as well as my own, once again, I thank you."

He stepped away from the microphone to applause somewhat warmer than polite, and shaking hands with Caldwell yet again, took his seat.

"And now, ladies and gentlemen," Caldwell began, "for the program in honor of our recipient . . ."

Well, it was a short speech, anyhow. Said the right things—thanks, humility, importance of the cause. What else was there? What else would they have wanted to hear? Aspirations? Ambitions? How longing for the Met—Broadway—even the band-

stand—faded with time? Vanished, at last—in the harsh light of limitation? The gulf. They have their own.

An acceptable, respectable speech. Proprieties observed. Polite. Refined. Competent. Comfortable. You are what you do—not what you might have done. "Kaddish for a Dead Dream." Intriguing title. Something to compose someday.

". . .verton playing the Liszt."

Mittelman's eye caught a door swing open at the rear. *Barbara.* She slid into a side-aisle seat under the applause greeting the pianist that Caldwell had just introduced. Smiling, she shook her head and shrugged. Mittelman returned the smile, nodding toward her in as the piece began.

She was good, very good, Yolanda Overton—technically proficient yet spirited. As she played, composition, instrument, artist fused—inseparable. There was uncompromised genius here. At the end, she accepted the long enthusiastic applause with deep bows and an open smile—radiance derived from unbanked fires within. Her encore, far more demanded than obligatory, was a polonaise of Chopin's played with joyful ease—more gift than obligation.

The quartet were nearly as good, confident, united in their common purpose and playing, perhaps a little too emphatic through the solo parts. But even that was exuberant, spontaneous. The cellist, Jaffe, was especially fine. He would likely find a chair someday with one of the principal orchestras—Cleveland—Philadelphia—and the other three—among the secondaries almost certainly, perhaps beyond.

But, Jaffe aside, they had not been his students, and even the cellist had been merely exploring a musical bypath. He did not turn out virtuosi, even musicians, in the narrow sense. No, his had been the world of cracked-voice, anxious or indifferent pubescents, though for years now the Bar Mitzvah teaching chores had been handled by his assistant or Hebrew School teachers. His had been and was the world of adult education and liturgical composition, helping to bind the people to their culture with the mortar of their evolving musical inheritance; his was the world of the school board meeting room, putting the case for musical life beyond the marching band. He had done the work of Telemachus. And these before him rising with instruments in hand were Ulysses.

Caldwell had returned.

"We come now to the final part of our program."

Mittelman collected himself in a meditative moment, rising to renewed applause with energy and clear purpose at the end of the introduction.

He had chosen the pieces with care, and, since it was not a formal recital, and because it was the Music Education Association that was honoring him, he prefaced each selection with a brief instructive comment.

"As many of you know, the art song is one of my favorite musical forms. This piece of Schubert's seems especially appropriate today in presenting the special claim of music as inspiration—a means of soaring beyond life's traumas. 'An die Musik'."

He felt enough of the solid baritone still there.

Not much range in the piece. A good warm up. A good reception.

"Thank you. Thank you very much. A little earlier you heard Mr. Caldwell refer briefly to my experience on the musical stage. He referred to it briefly because it was a brief experience. However that may be, the musical stage has long been a mainstay of popular culture. But sometimes the music transcends its medium—in Bernstein, to cite one example. Very often, it seems to me that the best of this music comes from the best book—Bernstein again, for example. I think the next song, not Bernstein's—illustrates this. Which of us, like Don Quixote himself, has not tilted at windmills? Has not dreamed an impossible dream?"

This was more difficult, the top a definite challenge. The voice grew thin, thinner but held. He bowed. Dabbed at his face with a handkerchief. Bowed again. A third time.

"Thank you. You are very kind."

He took a breath.

"My last piece is a little like the first. It too is about music, this time in Yiddish. Its subject is a kaptsn, a poor Jew, who though quarreling with God experiences miracle after miracle, "vunder iber vunder," when he sings.

More comfortable again. A brighter mood. An opportunity for some theatricality—if not quite Fiddler.

He hardly noticed the octave leap at the close although he cut the final note a beat short.

Mittelman bowed twice and retired from the stage. He returned to the sustained applause, retreated and returned once more to the scattered shouts of "Encore!"

He introduced and sang "Caro Mio Ben" Called back a second time, he offered a short satiric piece in French, "Le Petit Professeur." It was better than he had rehearsed it driving in.

They did not ask for a third. Still, he had acquitted himself well. Justice.

He remained in the wings as Caldwell thanked the audience for coming and invited them to the reception. Then, hearing the crowd dissolve in chatter and movement, Mittelman walked quietly out on stage and swiftly down the steps. Already, as if they were radiating from the island clusters gathering about the afternoon's participants, people were moving toward the various exits. Dozens of fellow students, a few faculty, and a parent or two surrounded the young musicians. Ebersole greeted a handful of colleagues, Caldwell a throng of Association members. Dr. Ranieri entertained a number of these as well, in addition to several school board representatives, family, and friends.

As he made his way toward the rear, a hand reached out here and there for his—Herron, the three cantors from Buffalo—though Rainer Sklar had apparently left, Mrs. Weil, Harriet Gorelik and Muriel, the Fergusons—all with a smile along with a "fine Job" "wonderful voice" or "Bravo!" from the uninitiated, or a nod of respect and understanding from the professionals.

"I hope I'm that good at sixty something," Goldhaber offered along with a lusty pat on the back.

"Still pushing the art song, I hear," Ross added, his jest bordering on jibe.

But spying his wife and sons at the rear, Mittelman abandoned his colleagues. Barbara kissed him lightly as they embraced.

"You were marvelous today, dear," she said with neither irony nor condition. "Sorry I missed your speech. I know that was wonderful too. But between the mist and the icing . . ." she sighed.

"You practically know the speech by heart," Mittelman reassured her. "Anyway, you're here now."

David broke in to hug him.

"Way to go, Dad. Say, let's see the plaque."

"As we say in Hebrew," Jordan gripped his father's arm and hand, "'May the force be with you'."

Laughing at his son's update of the traditional greeting, Mittelman nodded his thanks.

Barbara broke the silent pause that followed.

"Jordy's been telling me about a shoot he's beginning next week, an underwater feature about the renewal of Lake Erie."

"Only he's not the cameraman," David interrupted. "He's the mini-sub."

Jordan reached into his pocket for the borrowed cravat.

"Here's your tie," he said, looping it around his brother's neck in mock strangulation.

Barbara stopped the horseplay as she stepped between them.

"Now, be good boys and take me to the reception. I haven't eaten a thing since breakfast and I'm starving."

David and Jordan glanced at each other and sang "Yes, Mommy" in chorus.

Barbara and the young men made their way out. Mittelman followed, shaking his head and laughing softly.

In the reception room, the clusters of guests formed, dissolved, and formed again as if augmented and diminished by the rhythmic wash of the social sea. Mittelman navigated among them, touching here and there for an obligatory acknowledgment, the acceptance of yet another word of approval, thanks, or praise, then drifted off once more. He veered away once or twice from dervishing waiters, their canapé platters laden with rumaki. He noticed Barbara and the boys at the crowded main buffet; she was urging Jordan away from the empanadas and toward the ratatouille and crudités. The salmon mousse seemed appetizing—David was clearly enjoying his—and the miniature bagels studding the baskets otherwise piled with sourdough, petit pain and multi-grain rolls held the charm of the familiar in an exotic setting. At a side table, the desserts beckoned with customary allure. Harriet Gorelik recommended the kiwi tart and petits fours especially. Muriel concurred.

But he could eat nothing. He was satisfied. And this was not his milieu. With effort and experience he had long passed beyond mere civility at such gatherings to acquire a degree of grace. But it was far more labor than gift—not him, a bit of psychic falsetto. It was performance that was the life. There, to be among but not of was the norm. And even then, it was often less a matter of selfhood than transcendence—as if the music were all and he a mere vehicle. At times, it was as Ginzberg had said—he was the representative—no matter how unworthy. Those were the best times—and the times when, most perversely, he was most himself.

He stopped briefly before the bar, noting casually that the product of the small Finger Lakes vintners prevailed. It seemed appropriate.

"Herb!"

Goldhaber strode toward him, Ross and Immerglick in his wake.

"Where have you been hiding?"

Immerglick handed him a small folded slip of paper.

"From Sklar."

He read it and smiled.

"You must have one with us," Goldhaber commanded. He had already begun to pour.

"Cantor."

Mittelman turned to see Ehrlich offer a tentative hand, reserved as usual.

"May I wish you mazl tov, Herbert?"

"Don't ask permission. Wish!" Goldhaber commanded as he distributed the glasses.

"Mazl tov, then."

"Thank you, Elliot. Thank you very much," Mittelman replied, bowing slightly, stiffly from the waist as he shook Ehrlich's hand.

"Ehrlich. Herb, here's yours," Goldhaber completed his distribution.

"A—a toast?" Immerglick stammered.

After a moment of exchanged glances amid uncomfortable silence, Ross took over.

"What is there to say, after all? To Herbert Mittelman. L'khaim!"

"L'khaim!" came the chorus.

Mittelman slowly drained the baco noir, following it with his eyes as it passed between his lips. It seemed as if he were drinking his own life's blood shed in performance, now blessed, so to speak, by the affirmation and restored to him.

"Well, Mittelman, we must go," Goldhaber said, putting his own emptied glass aside. "It's a long drive," he added half-apologetically, "at least an hour and a half before all of us are home."

Immerglick took up the theme.

"And there's a threat of snow besides."

"A radical statement, Immerglick," Ross needled. "Valid only about ten months a year. Come."

He led Immerglick away, Goldhaber this time bringing up the rear.

"Have a safe trip," Mittelman called after them.

Ehrlich discarded his nearly full glass.

"I must be going too."

"I assume you have been invited to talk with Ranieri?"

"Yes."

"Good. Then I'll see you at the meeting next month."

"Yes. Good afternoon, Cantor."

"Good afternoon." He touched Ehrlich's arm lightly.

"Thanks for coming."

Ehrlich nodded, turned up one corner of his mouth uneasily, then left.

Many others had also gone—perhaps most. The islands of clustering bodies were now few and smaller. The debris of half-eaten food and soiled dishes seemed to cover tables like so much flotsam. Jordan and David came up to tell him that they were going home to catch what remained of the Browns game. Ranieri and Ebersole, leaving together, waved to him on their way out. Mazzoli and Siegfried were off in a corner—to judge by their motions, apparently in heated discussion of tempo—possibly for some piece they were preparing. The synagogue contingent, except for the two sisters still browsing among the desserts, had left half an hour ago.

But soon only he and Barbara, the catering staff, Dunstan Caldwell and his committee assistants remained. At last, these others also left, Caldwell with a word of polite praise to Mittelman himself and a more elaborate statement of her husband's virtues to Barbara.

Alone now, the pair stood together in the doorway, surveying the aftermath of celebration.

"Whose Bar Mitzvah was this?" Barbara quipped.

"I'm afraid it was a rite of a somewhat different kind," Mittelman said softly.

They looked at each other for a moment without speaking.

"I'll get our coats," he said.

Retrieving them, Mittelman helped Barbara with hers, then handed her the scarf and gloves.

"Oh, I forgot something."

"I'll wait in the hall."

Mittelman returned to the cloakroom and pressed a twenty into the departing hatcheck's hand.

On his way back, he paused at the reception room for a last look. It was empty, the rattling of dishes from the kitchen behind a sole sign of life. He buttoned his coat and rejoined Barbara, who stood between the inner and outer doors of the vestibule, gazing into the desolate parking lot.

She turned up his collar and kissed him.

"It looks awful," she said, nodding toward the blur of wet snow aswirl before the rising wind.

"The usual," he said.

Mittelman linked his arm with hers, and, bowing before the weather, stepped into the falling night.

Seascape

"Beautiful. Beautiful."
The words rose softly as sigh only to flutter down as silent mouthing.

Isadore Feinblum drew deliberate breath against the stiff sea breeze and continued watching the birds. Swoop, hover, and soar, gulls and pigeons passed above and below him. Once or twice, they seemed to hang suspended before the balcony on which he stood. So close, a daring man might lean over the wrought iron railing to touch them, thinking the effort worthwhile though destined to fail. Then they were off, pigeons to bare rooftops and cotes of squat, weathered buildings, gulls to the jetties or tide's edge or perhaps for a great arcing sweep of the visible sea. Just now, one had alighted atop a boardwalk fence post—a curve of thickened white against the steely, blue-gray angularities of intersecting planes—walk, water, and sky.

"Beautiful," Feinblum did not say again.

Perhaps it was the view, perhaps the still rising breeze, perhaps the falling temperature this late October afternoon—or all three—that set the old man shuddering. For an instant, his knees quivered and the day grew suddenly dark. He steadied himself against the railing with palm-sweated hands and recovered. Perhaps it was none of them.

"Dad? Dad, you all right?" Stuart Feinblum looked up from his magazine and peered anxiously through the open doorway.

His father nodded and forced himself to a hoarse "I'm fine."

"You don't sound so fine to me."

"How do I sound?

"Like you're catching cold again."

"As if, as if you're catching cold."

"Dad, you left the classroom six years ago."

"When I was seventy. Two years ago today I buried your mother. For a retired widower of seventy-six, I sound fine."

He wheezed catching his breath and coughed twice.

"At least put on a sweater. Remember what Greenbaum said."

"Greenbaum should treat animals. It would help control the pet explosion. A doctor should not smoke while discussing lung disease with his patients."

"Pneumonia is no joke, even without emphysema."

"Emphysema is no joke, even without pneumonia."

Feinblum returned to the living room, closing the door to the balcony behind him, his reverie and mood irreparably broken.

"Satisfied?" he asked, thin hands thrusting deep into the pockets of his baggy pants. Then, pacing slowly before the orderly but overflowing bookcase, he went on in mock-talmudic chant.

"Stuie, I want to make one thing perfectly clear. Your mother left you ten thousand dollars. Your mother left you the silver. Your mother left you the antique brass cuspidor you always liked. But your mother did not leave you her right to nudzh. That, my son, is a privilege of spouses only. Non-transferable. Fartik—done."

"Concern is not necessarily nudzhing."

"If I am not for me, who will be for me, and if not now, when?" Feinblum muttered.

"What?"

"I wasn't questioning your motives. Just the actions."

Injured and indignant, Stuart Feinblum tossed the magazine aside and raised his voice.

"Okay, so go back. I won't say a word."

"Too windy, "the father said, his smile as faint as it was fleeting.

"You are impossible."

They laughed together, their mingled sound momentarily salving all wounds, and, as they moved to the kitchen at the sound of the buzzing intercom, were spared an embarrassed silence that would have likely followed.

"Who is it?" Feinblum rasped.

"Yoshi."

"Can you manage?"

"Yes, Father, thank you. The boys are with me."

He pressed the lock release and went out to meet them at the elevator.

"So boys, how was the boardwalk?" he asked, as he took a package from their mother.

"Great, Grandpa. I beat Greg at Skee-Ball."

"Big whoop-de-do!" the older boy scoffed.

His brother answered the ridicule with a new challenge.

"Race you to the kitchen!"

They took off down the hall, bags of groceries cradled precariously in their arms.

"Nicky, the eggs!" their mother called in apprehensive pursuit.

Feinblum followed after and smiled.

"Good boys, fine boys," he thought, "my grandchildren without a doubt. But still . . ." he trailed off, shrugging.

"Alien," he might have continued. He had before. Their physical appearance was of no concern. What mattered were the miles that separated them, the 350 days a year or so they never met, the worlds within the sixty-odd years between their births. The blood bond was there; he had never denied it. But there were few others. One common language. Half a history. Celebrations, if you counted Thanksgiving and the Fourth of July. Passage rites, if you counted buying the first baseball glove and two-wheeler. Generation builds on generation brick by brick. But where was the mortar?

"Pass the peanut butter, wouldja?" Nicky whined at his bother.

The older boy scooped two fingers' worth from the open jar before sliding it across the formica tabletop.

The younger sneered in contempt.

His brother laughed and sucked at his hand obscenely.

"Have your snack, boys," their mother advised. We'll be leaving soon."

She had her back to them, busily, efficiently stocking Feinblum's refrigerator and cupboard shelves.

"All this should last you till after Thanksgiving," Yoshi said, as the old man entered the kitchen.

"Undoubtedly," Feinblum agreed, placing the bag he carried on a counter, "as more and more I am inclined to eat less and less."

She hesitated a moment, unscrambling the syntax, then admonished gently, "To diet is not to fast."

"Nor to feast, alas."

Stuart had joined them.

"You didn't do so bad—badly at lunch this afternoon."

"That was one instance and not typical. At times, Stuie, you confirm my belief that social scientists are not very scientific."

The younger Feinblum gnawed at the stem of his unlit pipe.

"If you must know, my virtuoso performance was the result of an irresistible combination of forces, to wit: pleasure, spite, obligation, and guilt."

"Tell us about it," Stuart humored him, pulling up a chair.

"Shall I lie down somewhere?"

"I'm an experimental psychologist, Dad, remember?"

"Shall I run a maze, then?"

"You are running one. Can you find your way back to the point?"

"Time me. Pleasure," he resumed at once, "because Horowitz has the best Rumanian pastrami to be had for fifty miles. Spite, because Greenbaum specifically forbade smoked meats. Obligation, because you were paying for it. Guilt, because a) I wouldn't have wanted to cause you worry by not eating, b) Greenbaum was right—for once, and c) pleasure is often proximal to sin. However, since I am likely to be ill by morning, atonement will have been made. As I am seventy-six, it will take me some time to recover from this afternoon's excesses. Therefore, I conclude that Yoshi has indeed bought enough food to last me beyond Thanksgiving."

"Thanksgiving's coming. Better watch it, turkey," Greg warned his brother.

In reply, Nicky sent the jar of peanut butter sliding toward him. With fine timing, and perverse grace, Greg in one motion thrust his slobbered fingers into the jar, dipped a second serving, and shot it back across the table.

"Nevertheless, Father, can I prepare some dinner for you," Yoshi offered, as she put away the last items and found a place for empty bags beneath the sink.

Feinblum declined the offer.

"No, thank you. No. Tonight I shall have my usual Sunday evening meal. An egg, a slice of toast, a cup of tea."

Nicky studied the moist prints in the peanut butter and looked up in disgust.

"You're gross!

His brother's grin widened.

"I thought you didn't like eggs," Stuart Feinblum considered.

"I don't," his father replied, "but since I've been allowed only three a week their taste has improved greatly. I think of them as a delicacy now, and, if not to be enjoyed exactly, to be experienced periodically, for reputation's sake. Scarcity, you know, determines worth, that and circumstance."

Feinblum moved toward the kitchen window and peered out at the waning day. Light faded steadily, and the sea rolled in softly or crashed upon the rocks at will, indifferent as if Canute himself had been there. A passing gull caught his eye.

"Take birds, for instance," he resumed, back still turned. "If you had asked me five years ago what seagulls meant to me, I would have said garbage dumps. Pigeons? Three ruined hats. But here, away from the city, they seem very different, our mirrors if you like. I have seen the entire cycle—birth, growth, mating, new birth, providing, quarreling, settling, death—I assume death, though I can't recall witnessing it—and between pigeons and gulls alone a range of styles, hierarchies, values. Self, nest, colony, cosmos. What does one emphasize? How much?

"A gull is an egotist, independent, skeptical—part of the colony, yes, but others had better keep their distance. It guards a nest as much to protect territory itself as to protect the young. Take that bird," he nodded, following a diminishing form through the dusk. "A lone gull, *lone*, not *lonely*. But if it were a pigeon, we would call it *stray*. Stray from what? From one other pigeon, at least. The species is utterly domestic—huddling, profuse, comfortable."

The seagull dissolved in blue evening. Feinblum, pausing for breath, turned from the window.

"It's fitting that Italians keep them—a robust, companionable people, with three generations to a house—or neighborhood at least. I mean the old Italians, like those two streets over, whose names still end in i's and o's.

"But here's a problem," he broke off abruptly and intense. "What if, having lived pigeonically (forgive the coinage), paired and public, one aspires to gullhood? And what if, given opportunity, gullhood is achieved, and that too is found wanting?"

He relaxed just as suddenly, shifting focus once again.

"Stuie," he mused, "has anyone at the university experimented with crossbreeding pigeons and gulls?"

"I don't talk to the aggies," Stuart mumbled, only half in jest, as he sucked to relight the dregs of his pipe.

Yoshi closed the freezer door for the last time.

"I've wrapped each chicken breast separately, Father."

Greg, who for the past three minutes had been gobbling derisively at his younger brother, now coughed and gagged on his father's pipe smoke.

"Stu, that smells like burnt feathers, "Yoshi scolded.

Feinblum spread his arms in mock despair.

"Chicken, feathers, turkey—I speak a little philosophy and get poultry in reply. A family of Philistines."

Stuart and Yoshi indulged him with polite laughter. The boys, startled at first, recovered, not much subdued.

"But now that I mention it," Feinblum resumed, following them all back to the living room as he spoke, "Socrates himself asked that a cock be sacrificed to Asclepius—after his death."

Catching his wife's eye, Stuart nodded toward the door.

"All right, Nicky, Greg," she clapped her hands. "Get your things."

Feinblum looked at his son, eyes questioning.

"We've got at least a three-hour drive, and the boys have school tomorrow, "Stuart observed without apology.

Feinblum nodded his expressionless assent. Amid the rustle and scuffling of departure, he took the barrel of taffy and the box of fudge from the coffee table.

"Gregory, Nicholas, don't forget these."

They came and shyly and performed their obligatory "thanksgrandpas."

Feinblum put an arm about each of them as they turned away. The boys looked back, wondering again at the unfamiliar touch.

"Remember, they're to be shared, Feinblum said, "and no quarreling or both of you will be 'gross turkeys'."

"He's the turkey," Greg pointed to his brother.

"And you're gross," Nicky hurled the gauntlet back.

They chased each other through the now open doorway and down the hall, candy tucked football fashion in the crook of one arm.

Feinblum shook his head in amusement.

"'Gross', 'turkey'," he thought to himself, "the 'now' version of 'oafish lout'."

"How will you spend the evening, Father," Yoshi asked, interrupting his reflection. "Aside," she teased, "from eating your gourmet dinner."

"I have no plans," he said. "Alvin, I suppose, will call at nine. Your brother is very predictable, Stuart. We speak every other Sunday evening without fail."

"Say hello to him for us."

"The telephone," Feinblum observed, "is a remarkably simple instrument to use."

Stuart Feinblum zipped his parka smartly. "We talked just before Labor Day," he half-barked through pipe-clenched teeth.

"And you saw each other the next week," Yoshi offered in bright appeasement.

"Oh, just for two minutes at the airport," Stuart responded to his father's surprise. "I had just arrived in New Orleans and he was heading back to Chicago, almost too late for the flight. He looked fine, said El and the kids were all right."

Feinblum recovered.

"What I have always admired most about the Renaissance is the ease with which a scribe, for example, might converse with a hawker of pies and he, in turn, with a keeper of dancing rats—even if they were not related—as they were not very likely to have been. Today, poet and journalist, swine seller and dairyman, fencing master and football coach scarcely acknowledge each other's existence, even if they are identical twins."

Stuart Feinblum colored.

"Dad, Al lives about eight hundred miles away. He is a broker on a commodities exchange, whose workings I understand as little as he understands a laboratory. And though it should matter less than it used to, he is eight years older than me."

"I."

"I," the younger Feinblum shouted, then controlled himself at his wife's signal.

"But, father, what will you do until Alvin calls?" Yoshi ventured, at once defusing the moment further and returning Feinblum's focus to the topic of her earlier question.

"I'll nap after dinner," he obliged, "then attempt to amuse myself with the radio, phonograph, or if sufficiently desperate, the television set. I dislike one-way communication—a contradiction in terms. At times I understand how my students must have felt when I lectured instead of teaching. After your brother-in-law calls, I might take the papers to bed."

"I notice," Stuart remarked, "that there are three issues of the *English Teachers' Journal* still in wrappers on the coffee table."

"I hardly look at them these days," Feinblum sighed, "but I almost can tell you the contents. "Shakespeare for the Underachiever." One dare not say 'illiterate'. "Building a Guillotine: An Affective Approach to *A Tale of Two Cities*."

No, thank you, I would rather fiddle with the dials than observe civilization decline with—how did Frost put it—'the slow, smokeless burning of decay'."

"MomDadMomDadMomDad!" Greg and Nicky's wail echoed their impatience down the corridor.

"We'd better go, Dad, "Stuart said. "Remember to come up the week before."

He backed toward the elevator, waving as he spoke.

"Call us about the flight."

"Goodbye, Father," Yoshi said. She touched Feinblum lightly on both shoulders and kissed his cheek.

"Goodbye, boys," he called to his grandsons.

Their repeated "byegrandpas" resounded through the hall until their father drew them, half struggling, into the elevator.

Closing the door behind him, Feinblum drank deeply of the sudden hush, honeyed now for all the bitterness it would bear an hour hence. He crossed to an armchair grown oversized and settled in silence to watch the very last of twilight, phantom day easing soundless into peaceful dark. Then, faintly through window and wall, coming as if from horizon's edge, a single cry of a seagull. Darkness, and then the ruffle and coo of pigeons at roost in the snug of evening. Forgoing his planned repast and half curling about himself, Feinblum slept.

The telephone awakened him. He stirred, unfurled himself with care, and reached for the lamp. The phone rang a fourth time. He studied the clock above the bookcase.

"It's probably Alvin," Feinblum mumbled as he rose.

Shuffling and coughing his way across the room, he picked up at the seventh ring.

"Hello."

"Yes. Hello, Alvin."

"No, I was just dozing."

"It's all right. If I had slept on, I would have been up half the night. How are you?"

"Good. How are Elaine and—the children?"

"I'm pleased to hear it. Although Stuart told me as much."

"Stuart—your brother."

"Yes, New Orleans."

"They're all well. Stuart sends his regards."

"I'll do that, but I believe that I last worked for Western Union sixty years ago."

"Yes, if I visit for Thanksgiving I will see him before you will. But you needn't dispatch a personal emissary to deliver the message."

"I know you are—both of you. But as the poet says, 'The world is too much with us; late and soon, /Getting and spending, we lay waste our powers'."

"No. Wordsworth."

"Am I keeping busy? That depends on whether you perceive activity from a Newtonian or Einsteinian point of view."

"Newtonian. I might have guessed as much. In that case, yes, I keep busy. I stroll the boardwalk in good weather, nod at familiar faces, chat with my old colleague Rosoff if I meet him, sit on the benches with my contemporaries, and stare at them as they stare at the sea."

"Not at all, Alvin. I'm disinterested, a student. I study them as I do the birds from my balcony. Each is a means of knowing myself."

"Socrates, yes."

"Not any more. I've given up tutoring."

"I tried it again for the first month of this semester, but the futility of it was overwhelming. Imagine, adults who hardly know the alphabet, struggling to read well enough to get a decent job, a job that will be filled or phased out by the time they can read fluently or for which they will then be too old."

"No, Alvin. I am not above it. I am, I fear, beyond it."

"My status otherwise is quo. Greenbaum continues to present me with a dirty bill of health, and Mrs. Kern still pays me fruitless court with her home-made morsels, which, if consumed, would soil Greenbaum's bill the more."

"Alvin, I would expect you, of all people, to be realistic. I take her less seriously than I take Greenbaum, if that is possible. What makes you think differently?"

"Yes, I know what today is. How could I forget?"

"Did you? I felt no need. Perhaps I myself was the memorial candle."

"I grant you that the image might be maudlin; nevertheless, the substance is fact."

"No, I won't spend the week burdening Stuart and Yoshi with my self-indulgence—if I go."

"I plan to, but plans change."

"Gang aft agley."

"Gang aft agley. It's Scots dialect."

"Yes, that's what it means."

"It's fitting that Burns is quoted on the exchange. He was a farmer.

"Why so early?"

"Does one look forward to a sunrise flight to Des Moines? It does not smack of adventure and romance."

"Yes, as you say, there are things each of us must do. I'll let you go. Say hello to everyone for me."

"Yes, I'll speak with you before Thanksgiving. Have a good trip, and thanks for calling."

"Goodbye, Alvin."

"'Amid the alien corn,'" Feinblum murmured as he lowered the receiver, "though hardly 'sick for home.'"

He walked away and wandered aimlessly about the apartment. Although he had not known it long, he knew it to the very blemishes. It was a kind of domestic gallery, revisited less for the familiar works themselves than for assurance that they still were there. Yes, there was the crack along the foyer baseboard, the bathroom ceiling stain where Milner's tub had overflowed and faucet handles both marked "C," a bit of paint chipped from the bedroom doorjamb and, within, the bed crisply made under Yoshi's hand but whose mattress remained depressed on the one side on which he continued to sleep, a bit of exposed kitchen switch plate free of an otherwise uniform beige, a thin scratch along the edge of the refrigerator door.

Minutes later, Feinblum was back in the living room, seated in the armchair once again, fortified against the night with a cup of warmed milk and the *Times* magazine. He sipped as he leafed through, glancing at advertisements, reading a caption.

He paused at the page marked "Interiors," brows raised and nostrils flaring. After all, wasn't it always the same design, perhaps rotated ninety degrees, or with an L bent alternately left and right, or unchanged but newly furnished, or photographed from different angles with the same appointments, perhaps some combination of these? He had always wondered how it was done. Within, there seemed to be no walls—just spaces—floating, flowing into each other—kaleidoscopic, yet finite, so that no matter what the arrangement or furniture, the plan evoked a recurring sense of déjà vu from week to week.

Looking up, Feinblum rolled the still warm cup between his fingers and considered his own room. Closed except for the foyer archway and broad balcony window whose drapes he had not drawn. Unchanging except for the now invisible sea. He nodded approvingly, having achieved, he thought, as much as the architects and with less trouble. Stasis—the first law of inertia.

There were his records, for instance, now seldom played, or when played, hummed to—they were so familiar—Telemann, Haydn, Mozart—so that they were not heard, or if heard, unheeded as sounds of ordinary life. Or of extraordinary life, as of, say, the mechanical companion, staring blankly like some gray-eyed Polyphemus in the farthest corner. Rosoff and Mrs. Kern, he knew, watched soap operas and court shows—or turned them on even when out of the room—far less for amusement than for the illusion of human voices. If an imitation of an imitation is twice removed from reality, how remote is an imitation of a non-imitation?

He glanced toward his copy of *The Republic*. Dust lay thick upon it, shadowing the shadows of the cave. Others too stood untouched for months, for years. He knew them all. Doubtless, Emma Bovary still died writhing by her own hand; Lear of grief resulting from his own foolishness; and through perversity of man and God, Moses, the great teacher, come to know but visions of a promised land.

Above the books in a simple frame—less covered with dust— Sylvia smiled familiarly. He had known her—once and long—to the subtlest mark, manner, mood. He knew that smile still, alike in adversity and joy, bearing the one with patience, the other with grace. So had she smiled walking a deserted beach one early May evening when they first were told. And then, as now, the words leaped to mind unbidden, unspoken, yet tallying the handclasp and silent gaze he had returned: ". . . the sea/Delaying not, hurrying not, /Whisper'd me through the night and very plainly before daybreak/Lisp'd to me the low and delicious word death/ And again death, death, death, death . . ."

Undressed for bed, Feinblum listened for the rush of waves upon the jetties, the pulsed pause and gathering rumble of return. He heard only the distant moaning in spaces between soughs of wind. Surely, the tide was out.

Toward morning, Feinblum discovered himself upon the balcony, beckoning the pigeon flock and scattered, hovering gulls with silent mouthings. He leaned far over the railing, then raised his arms to them in the long moment of his soaring. With unuttered cries of warning, they sheared off. He fell slowly in empty-armed anguish. Then it was dark. He did not move as the crowd gathered round him.

A Sage in Israel

Gershon Richter placed a small silver tray on the table beside his armchair and carefully poured himself a cup of tea. He added a level teaspoon of sugar, stirring it in slow, deliberate circles, silent. Then, easing himself into the chair and gazing into a dimly lit corner of the study, he spoke as if resuming a suspended conversation.

"So, when were you not a skeptic? If you could have spoken at your own bris, you would have protested the ritual's pagan origin, no doubt citing historical and anthropological evidence in support of your contention.

"Still," Richter mused, 'I witnessed the circumcisions of both your sons, being honored as sandek for the younger."

He took some tea, dissolved a crumb of cake in his mouth, and drank again.

"I did say *skeptic*, not *scoffer*. Smile, yes, smile. But you know it's true."

He sipped once more, his eyes making a slow sweep of the room before him as he savored the faintly sweet mouthful. It was a comfortable study, the carpet thick, the chairs amply padded, the oak of the bookshelves and half-paneling darkened with age. The well-used books themselves were in orderly array, sacred separate from secular, though less in opposition than in mutually catalytic counterpoise. For Richter, however, the question was one of just proportion, not equality, and works of faith and tradition outnumbered the rest.

"As for ritual, Richter began again, replacing the cup and saucer as he spoke, "your objections were already of long standing."

He laughed to himself quietly and close-mouthed.

"I remember your father, may he rest in peace, pleading with you to break the glass at your wedding, and how you protested that you had no need to ward off the devil or the evil eye.

"The adamance of youth," Richter sighed, and then returned to his subject.

"Even if the origin was in such medievalism, five centuries of associating the broken glass with the remembrance of Jerusalem and the Temple should have sufficed for reason. But not for you. Not for Judah Neufeld, purist!"

He regained control.

"Forgive me. You are, of course, my guest.

"Yet you did it, after all," Richter continued, pouring a little fresh tea into the nearly full cup, for the moment too disturbed by his own outburst to look up. "And, if I may say so, because I proposed you do it to preserve shalom bayit. So you did it, yet saved intellectual face.

"I can't say I was surprised by your, forgive me again, willfulness. The tendency was always there."

Richter fingered the rim of the cup, then, edging forward, spoke at more familiar ease.

"Do you remember the time your refused to participate in the Purim festival. Yes, you agreed, a masquerade was appropriate for the occasion, because Esther and Mordecai were just masks for the pagan deities Ishtar and Marduk. And the grager you denounced that year as 'the bullroarer of Babylon'—a nice ring that phrase. I have often wondered though," he mused as he broke another morsel of cake, "whether your opposition then extended to hamantashen as well."

There was no reply, but for Richter, Neufeld's face, still smiling, seemed to validate the small joke and signal the assent of its victim. Richter himself chuckled, then took the bit of cake he had just broken and drank deeply of the tea.

"Still," he continued, "this was nothing compared to your vehemence against the rite of the lulav and etrog. When the topic is sexual, may the Holy One preserve us, there is no telling to what heights passions—so to speak—may be roused. Perhaps you were, as my grandchildren would say—may the Holy One preserve them— 'uptight' about the subject.

"In any case, according to Judah Neufeld, disciple of the sage of Vienna, the tapering palm leaf wrapped with myrtle and willow is phallic, the oval citron its female counterpart, their being joined, shaken, and thrust toward the four quarters a kind of simulated copulation.

"So, when did I deny it?"

Richter stood, gathered the tea things on their tray and bore them to the glass-topped desk in the corner behind him, speaking over his shoulder as he went.

"However, the point is not copulation but simulation. Not the act but its significance."

He placed the tray and turned back.

"How is it," he went on with increasing vigor, "that you have always confused the object and its referent? Yes, it is sexual. Yes, it is a fertility rite. But is not the first commandment, long before the Decalogue, 'Be fruitful'? And isn't fruition development, first of individuals, then of their relationships, then of the children of Israel collectively, and ultimately of all human kind? And must we not fulfill this commandment before we can in sanctity perform the second—'and multiply'?

"And how better to depict these truths than in performing such a ritual during the harvest season? But the rite itself remains, like all rites, an emblem or representation, not essence."

Evening had begun to fall, and as Richter spoke, a cloud passed before the dimming sun, casting for a long moment a troubling shadow upon Neufeld's now more somber visage.

Richter ended his harangue and raised his hands, gesturing as if to pacify his companion. Then he turned on the desk lamp and, sitting at the edge of the desk, palms pressed lightly upon it, spoke quietly, warmth and humor returning to his voice.

"You know, Yehuda, we have been good for each other all these years. The Talmud instructs us to study at least in pairs, so that we may see the truth through eyes other than our own, to see that we seldom see the truth unaided. And what could have been more humbling for each of us than to have the other, the diametric other, for his study mate? Could old Hegel himself have devised a more graphic illustration of thesis and antithesis than the two of us? But," he considered, "for all our debate, argument, and counter, I have not seen the synthesis—unless it was just that—the two of us."

He rose and moved with measured pace toward the shelves that held his sacred texts.

"Our problem, undoubtedly, has been one of differing premises. You have always maintained that we are rational beings created in the image of a rational deity. I have held, on the contrary, that while we are capable of approaching the image of our creator, we are also subject to purely human urges, emotions, desires, which are intrinsically irrational and which must be controlled. Ritual is a means of such control, totally self-consistent, functioning as a rule and model for that internal resolve which may be insufficient or absent without it. You see us as perfected but marring our perfection by clinging to superstition; I see us as perfectible and striving toward perfection by means of our varied usages."

Richter paused, reflecting for an instant upon his own rhetoric.

"'Perfected', 'perfectible'. Has more than a half-century's debate depended on the difference between two suffixes?"

He dismissed the momentary doubt.

"But what a difference! Wise fools that we are, we have the same destination but can't agree on how far it is, or how to get there—or even where we are right now.

"To continue then," he pressed on and removed a thick volume from its shelf.

"As usual, I can support my case with the history of—don't wince—sacrifice. Even if the Temple had not been destroyed, sacrifice would have fallen into disuse. As early as Genesis 22 we have evidence of the rejection of human sacrifice in the story of Abraham and Isaac, in which the Holy One himself provides a ram as substitute. Again, in Leviticus 18 and 20 we twice have the proscription against sending children to the fires of Molokh. Already we have the thread of humanism not only in reverence for human life generally, but for the lives of children in particular. Compared even to Hellenic perspectives of a roughly equivalent period, in the matter of Agamemnon and Iphigenia, for example, this is truly enlightened.

"Jephthah and his daughter? Will you challenge me with that abomination? It is as exceptional to our practices, ancient and modern, as it is unlawful. Still, no deity demands the girl's blood, and the father weeps, after the fact, at his own rashness—perhaps that is your parallel to the Greeks here. Besides, it is possible that the child was not sacrificed but cloistered instead. Yes, revolting still, but perhaps less revolting.

"But I know you, Yehuda Neufeld," Richter went on, now winking and wagging a playful finger as he spoke, "you and your bogey man of a Jephthah.

Do you think I've forgotten the time your teenage Rachel came home half an hour late on a Saturday night? 'Sit down, Rokhl,' you said, 'let me read you a bedtime story.' And so you read the latter part of Judges 11. And at the last verse, with the daughters of Israel lamenting the daughter of Jephthah, Rachel collapsed on the couch of exhaustion—and boredom—but you, thinking you had gone too far, began shaking her and calling for smelling salts until Anna convinced you that she was simply sleeping.

"You let her stay on the couch all night, fetching the blankets yourself and propping her head on a pillow. Haven't I always said your virtues were charity and mercy?"

Richter resumed his argument, all amusement fading from his face.

"Jephthah aside, then, no doubt you will tell me that animal sacrifice persists and is preserved throughout the scriptures, from the daily offering to the paschal lamb to the scapegoat for Azazel on Yom Kippur, but haven't we since the earliest rabbinic times construed sacrifice as a giving of our selves or goods or time to our fellow creatures? And even in the case of atonement, we must first ask and receive forgiveness of our fellows before we can ask it of the One on high. Thus, as we have grown increasingly humane in these respects, the ancient practices, no longer essential as guides, have fallen into disuse.

"Yet you will tell me that our prayer books still retain accounts of animal sacrifice and that dietary laws still require ritual slaughter of permitted animals.

"To the first I say, one cannot know where he is unless he knows where he has been. To the second, restricting slaughter to the trained and chosen few, not only absolves us collectively of the taint of blood, but also removes us from immediate suggestions of bloody thoughts or deeds. Ancient rites recalled and modern ritual slaughter both preserve the community—one by historical ties—one by civilizing distance from an act that performed indiscriminately, casually, and repeatedly, might easily defile and dehumanize the spirit."

Richter drew a deep breath and leafed through the volume in his hand. He stopped to hold a random place with his forefinger, then closed the book upon it, clutching the text as if for moral support in the difficult argument to come.

"I know, I know," he began again, gesturing for silence with his free hand. "You will seize upon the word *permitted*. Why, given the benevolence of the creation, are some species forbidden as unclean? In the case of predators and scavengers, the prohibition against blood applies—even at second remove. You, of all people, must admit the logical consistency of that," Richter added, appealing to his adversary's uncompromising rationalism.

"In regard to swine, shellfish, and the rest, we are agreed that questions of intrinsic repulsiveness, health, and sanitation are beside the point. So, why then? As my grandfather might have said," he grinned, 'So then, why not?' But," he shook his head, "you will not accept the justice of that response. Yet it has some merit."

Book still in hand, Richter began pacing slowly, steadily, between the shelves and his desk.

"The forbidden foods are to us what the tree of knowledge was to Adam and Eve, a test of will, of self-control, an impediment to the arrogant assumption that all creation is at our disposal. In short, a means of establishing integrity—not only within each of us but among us all. And this is why, though the prohibitions are arbitrary, as, indeed, all standards are (since the rationale typically follows their establishment), we cannot individually reject any commandment or substitute one of our own devising. For, while this might satisfy a private notion of purity, it destroys the collective standard, abolishes, in fact, the very idea of standard, since practices then would not be matters of common consent and would therefore, subject us to a moral Babel, incoherent and truly irrational.

"No, Judah Neufeld, you may not forgo brisket for lobster, as you have so often threatened to do, without weakening the bonds between yourself and your brethren, without straining the fibers of your own being, by so facile a denial of denial."

Richter stopped his harangue, but continued with a touch of quiet mischief in his voice.

"You see, it does not matter whether the swine is totem or taboo. As long as," he added in underscoring earnest, "unity of spirit, identity of spirit, is achieved."

Richter restored the book to its shelf, his disquisition for the moment completed. He returned to his chair and sat leaning forward on the edge of the cushion, imploring and intimate.

"But why do I argue with you? Why do I labor to convince you, when your whole practice affirms what your head and tongue alone deny? Have I ever known you to sow a field with two different kinds of seed, plough with a mixed team of ox and ass, to wear garments blended of linen and wool? Haven't you always maintained kashres? What were all those underlinings in the travel guides—'dietary laws observed'? Haven't you kept the Passover? What were those matse crumbs in the folds of your briefcase from Pesakh to Pesakh? Yet always murmuring, always doubting, always protesting, acting as if under duress. It was as if you would keep the ways of the Holy One, yet, like Job, maintain your own ways before Him.

"To my grandmother, who had a nickname for everyone, you might have been "Yehuda Why." An apt sobriquet. For Judah Neufeld there is no response that does not provoke another question. You have been a challenge. A definite challenge. And for sixty years you have taken my soul."

Richter eased himself toward the back of the chair. He sighed once, deeply, but with no sound other than the passage of breath.

"And finally," he resumed quietly, "to the question of miracles. Yes, yes, the most distasteful subject of all. But notice," he remarked, half in provocative jest, "the tripartite division of my argument—coherent, balanced, incremental—such as you might have chosen yourself. The one thing we have always agreed on is the protocol of our disagreement."

"Creation," Richter considered, hands clasped across this stomach, "is always synthetic, regardless of whether the result is a tangible object or an abstract idea. But the creation is a series of syntheses, which in fact, also constitute analysis. Here the Holy One reveals Himself through and as the totality of being, as if the ineffable whole may be perceived (as is the case) only through the sum of its manifested parts. For, as the psalmist states in the preferable translation, 'the earth is of the Lord and the fullness thereof', that is, not only emanating from the divine source but retaining the divine impulse in its being.

"Yet the creation is not in itself divine; it is worthy of admiration, not adoration. For our faith not only rejects idolatry but affirms the uniqueness of the Creator: 'Hear O Israel, the Lord our God, the Lord is one.' That is to say, not only is there none other, even the works of His own hands, but also that all is subsumed by His unity.

"However, why should this One create, become multiple in His manifestation?"

Richter leaned forward in his seat, pumping his arm forth and back from the elbow as if holding the essence of his argument between the pinched thumb and forefinger of his closed hand.

"And this, Yehuda, is the crux, the very miracle. Because in the creation divinity comprehends itself, becomes comprehensible in its comprehensiveness. Surely, there is nothing more awesome than the supreme analysis which leads to the supreme fulfillment of the Supreme Being."

Richter stood, as if raised by the force of his own peroration.

"Unless, of course, it's your tolerating so much metaphysics."

Nodding in amused satisfaction with this last remark, he crossed to the window and with hands folded behind him stared briefly into the gathering dusk. Then, he looked toward Neufeld's corner, darkened now not only by the rush of evening but also by his own eclipsing of what light remained.

"You would rather talk—how do you say it—nuts and bolts—by which you mean—sex. An unfortunate figure of speech."

Richter turned back toward the window.

"It is simple enough. Sexuality is but a refinement of the analysis. Incorporating all, divinity must be, as the kabbalists knew, androgynous. It is implicit in Genesis 1:27-''and God created man in His own image, in the image of God create He him; male and female created He them'—where *man*, to be sure, is generic. But it is clearer still in Genesis 2: 20-24, the story of the rib, in which the Almighty is conscious that the analysis is not complete, for the man, specific now, is alone. The use of the rib stresses not only the union of the sexes but their union in the godhead as well, since the surgery does not result in a new species but in completion of the divine image already sketched in the male. The passage, you recall, ends with the phrase 'and they shall be one flesh,' which emphasizes the unity in diversity exhibited by the Creator generally.

"The creation of man, then, to the extent that man is created in the divine image, is a microcosm of the creation as a whole. Having looked inward for five days, the Holy One sought a mirror on the sixth.

"Yes, Yehuda, you would add that it is no wonder he rested on the seventh.

"As for that, it is a wonder that you acknowledge the 'days' of creation at all."

Richter circled the room as he spoke, pausing behind his chair to switch on the floor lamp. The space was half suffused with soft light, which, paradoxically, cast Neufeld's corner into deeper gloom; yet the contrast seemed harmonious, necessary, the Yin and Yang of illumination and shadow in the little cosmos of the study.

"But even the pious and learned have made their peace with Darwin. And, as you would say, when a day might be ten billion years, when Methuselah could live to be 969, and when an eight o'clock appointment means 9:30—give or take—it is clear that the universe runs on Jewish time."

Richter sat again, peering alertly into the dusk of Neufeld's corner.

"On the surface, no doubt, the miracles of the Exodus seem less benevolent. But a principle of justice, strict justice, if you will, underlies them all. Each of the plagues, for instance, may be ascribed to Pharaoh's stubborn refusal to free the Israelites, and the last, poetic justice here, has the first born of the Egyptians dying, even as the first born among the Hebrews had been killed upon Pharaoh's command. But observe the distinction: the royal decree is arbitrary, political, genocidal in intent; the divine decree is retributive, moral, and consequent upon a series of pharaonic refusals to do justice.

"Again, each plague creates an ecological imbalance, whether in the form of natural disaster or disease. But here again the imbalance is a reflection and consequence of a corresponding imbalance in the human ecosystem, namely the enslavement of the children of Israel by the Egyptians. Nor is the material manifestation of moral decadence an exclusively biblical theme. Consider, for example, the *Oedipus Rex*, with Thebes plague-stricken for harboring the guilty Oedipus in its midst.

"But to return—even the crossing of the Red Sea reflects the disruption. Significantly, once the Israelites cross and are literally free of Egypt and bondage, the sea resumes its natural state and, ironically, destroys the pursuing Egyptians. For those who thrive in a parasitic system should rightly suffer when that system is destroyed.

"Yet, Yehuda, you object, on what you call humane grounds, to these sufferings divinely inflicted. But weigh, Yehuda, the weeks or months or years of travail against the generations and centuries of enslavement. And consider, Yehuda, who it is that emphasizes the plagues in themselves, the untutored, the popular mind.

"Among the Buddhists, as you well know, worship has a greater and a lesser form. The latter is, by our lights, mere idolatry, the other, an aspiration toward the metaphysical and the abstract, toward first principles. So too with the plagues. The idolatrous stop at representation, at the events themselves; the philosophical ask their significance.

"You have read the Pesakh Haggadah."

Richter paused, considered his needless understatement, then exclaimed:

"Have you read the Pesakh Haggadah! Every paragraph a matter for disputation! Is it right to make children squirm so, my humanist? And your Anna has horror tales of cold soup and burnt roasts to curl the hair of a bald gourmet. Though, to defend you—what am I saying—among us cosmopolites 10:30 is a very fashionable hour to dine!

"But," he resumed, his tone more reserved even as he warmed to the argument, "you have indeed read the Haggadah and well know that the space given to the plagues is proportional to that given to the history of the Exodus as a whole. It is the benevolence and might of the Holy One that is stressed. As for suffering, the matzoh itself, after all, is the bread of affliction, and the first response to the child's four questions concerning the difference between the night of Passover and all others begins with 'Because we were slaves in Egypt.' The first cause, if you like.

"Moreover, even in the midst of celebrating our release, we symbolically diminish our joy while recounting the plagues suffered by the Egyptians. The second of our four cups of wine is not drunk full, since before drinking it we spill a drop for each plague mentioned. Likewise, since all plagues cease with the Exodus, no further punishment is wreaked upon Egypt. For with the end of enslavement, the state of moral health, and, therefore—metaphorically—physical well-being, is restored."

He paused to brush a remnant cake crumb from his lap then continued speaking as if there had been no interruption.

"Perhaps more remarkable, however, is that after the Exodus alliances between Egyptians and the children of Israel were ultimately permitted with offspring in the third generation eligible for membership in the sacred assembly. All this by way of acknowledging Egypt's initial hospitality. The delay, I suspect, was less to allow the more recent and long-standing animosities to cool than to purge the Israelites of all vestiges of slave mentality and so enable them to deal with their counterparts as equals."

Richter smiled wistfully. "Would that you and I had such a—rapprochement. Azoy," he added, the familiar Yiddish "just so" at once confirming the sentiment and serving as self-reproach for affecting the borrowed French.

"All right, all right, Yehuda," he went on, as if chastened by his friend's gaze. "From now on nothing but plain English."

He rose again as he spoke and sidled toward the shelves of his secular library.

"Has it occurred to you, Yehuda," he continued," that like Passover the message of Khanuka is the restoration of collective identity? To be sure, we dwell on the rededication of the Temple and particularly on the story of a day's worth of oil that burned for eight. But the eternal light was the heart of the Temple, as the Temple itself was—is—you have been to the wall and seen—

"No," he protested, raising both his hands, "I want to hear nothing of your winter solstices and parallels to the Yule log and Christmas tree. Naturally, I expect that you have objections—on rational and scientific grounds no less—to the oil's burning for eight days. No doubt you will tell me that one of the politically and psychologically astute of the Maccabees, Jonathan perhaps, gave the story out as a kind of public relations puffery.

"Maybe so—don't be shocked that I agree with you. I assure you it is only for a moment. Perhaps then, it was a bit of Maccabean propaganda. The point is irrelevant— the moment has passed you see—irrelevant because the story succeeded in uniting an all but demoralized people long subject to Greco-Syrian despotism. And," Richter added, raising his hand as if to halt Neufeld once again, "do not be too eager to condemn as specious the solidarity based upon fabrication. For the literal falsehood, assuming it was such, is insignificant beside the spiritual truth conveyed. Another metaphor," he observed in wry conclusion, "the steel-edged mind defeated once more by poetry."

Richter turned to slowly scan the shelves behind him, took a small volume from one of them, and turned back. He leafed through the text without hesitation, knowing precisely where to find the passage he sought.

"Yes, Yehuda, you would find the Maccabean ruse more fraudulent than miraculous. But hear what an eminent church authority—albeit a fictional one—has to say. *Saint Joan*, Act II, scene 2," Richter stretched the syllables as he spoke, eyes and fingers searching the exact lines.

"Ah—the Archbishop of Rheims. 'A miracle, my friend, is an event which creates faith. That is the purpose and nature of miracles. They may seem very wonderful to the people who witness them, and very simple to those who perform them. That does not matter; if they confirm or create faith. they are true miracles.' And one speech later he adds: 'Frauds deceive. An event which creates faith does not deceive: therefore, it is not a fraud but a miracle.' So for the book of Shaw."

Richter closed the volume silently and returned it to the shelf. Night had fallen now, and he moved softly toward Neufeld's darkened corner to turn on the table lamp beside the green tufted club chair. Subdued by an amber shade, the light spread toward the brighter pool created by Richter's desk and floor lamps but failed to reach it, leaving a broad, black, arcing swath between them.

"This," Richter said, tapping the shade as he spoke, "is not a miracle. The light of the Maccabees is, as are, with apologies to the Archbishop, such events as ritual slaughter, sacrifice, and the superficially heathenish heaving of citron and leaves."

Richter breathed deeply as he passed behind the table and chair.

"A neatly rounded conclusion, don't you think?"

For an instant, a vague tremor at the upturned corners of his mouth belied the fervent bravado of his speech.

"But," he went on, "what do these and all the rest imply? A sense of solidarity, communion, oneness. An affirmation that we are not alone, separate, isolated specks in a meaningless universe. Even prayer—yes—prayer, perhaps especially prayer!"

His voice had risen as he spoke to an emphasis verging on tirade. At the end, he stood in the shadow between the two illumined spaces, staring hard and earnestly toward Neufeld.

"Tell me, Yehuda, what was it that the martyrs from Akiba to the six million proclaimed at their deaths? The Shema! 'Hear, O Israel, the Lord our God, the Lord is One.' And what was it that so many of the same six million chanted on their way to martyrdom? Ani ma'amin—'I believe with perfect faith that the Messiah will come, even though he tarry.' Can you deny these acts of prayer are miracles? Still, Yehuda, even still, does your head do battle with your heart?"

For a moment, silent now, Richter held his posture of challenge. Then his body grew slack. He passed from shadow to light as he crossed slowly into his own portion of the room. Back turned, he rested a hand upon the leather chair then spoke, haltingly at first, as if bemused.

"Yet they were six million—after all—and the martyred rabbis. But we—I—still, one is permitted to pray alone—if he must. You will forgive me this, Yehuda, as you have before. Your perversity has never been a match for your compassion. It is my need."

Slowly sliding his hand from the chair, Richter moved more slowly still behind the desk, withdrew a small box of matches and a wax-filled tumbler from the bottom drawer, then walked back through the swath of shadow to the mantle. Placing the tumbler in a silver filigree holder, he struck the match, touched it to the wick, and watched as the flame steadied from flare to restless flicker. The light encroached feebly upon the dark space between the armchairs in irregular waves, narrowing it, now more, now less, but never achieving more than momentary erosion.

Richter played his fingers over the silver work even as the light played upon his face, and whispered softly.

"Only the best, Yehuda."

He turned and moved in methodic half-shuffle past the night-blackened window. His voice, still hushed, hovered between argument and supplication.

"There is no harm, Yehuda, in the Mourner's Kaddish. No mention of death or afterlife. Simply affirmation of faith, acknowledgment of divine benevolence, acceptance of cosmic inevitabilities—if not quite in the manner of your Lucretius. On occasion, you have uttered the words yourself. What matter that I lack a minyen? That I am not obliged?"

His voice rose now.

"There are bonds beyond blood! Stickler! Will you torment me still with the letter of the law?"

In his passion, Richter strode toward Neufeld, reaching as if to seize him. Then subsiding almost at once, he lowered his arms, nodded, and returned the faint, familiar smile.

"As I have said," he whispered, "you are my guest."

Adjusting his skullcap and turning to face the study's eastern wall, Richter began the Kaddish prayer: "Yisgadal, v'yiskadash, sh'mey rabo"—eyes shut, face contorted in fervor, rocking rhythmically from the waist as he chanted.

Still smiling benignly, Neufeld stared ahead from the table beside the club chair, motionless.

Leybele Klein

At the funeral of Leybele Klein neither his widow nor his children grieved excessively, their mourning de rigueur, more formal than felt. But the sparse attendance, a dozen or so scattered throughout the oversized chapel, was depressing. And the eulogy, delivered by a nephew of the funeral director, proved an embarrassment beyond the relief of its own unintended comedy.

Leybele Klein, "devoted husband and father," had dealt kindly with neither wife nor child. He had been reluctant to marry in the first place, and only the necessity of a helpmeet had driven him to the canopy at last. If he had been at all drawn to Jennie by his senses, the lure was neither lip nor limb nor eye, but a stout, broad back and the healthy lungs concealed beneath it. There had been no question of the heart.

For six years before the crash of '29, Jennie had labored a ten-hour day in Klein's neighborhood hardware store, lugging gallons of paint and sacks of sand, joyless but without complaint. Klein had worked beside her but was often called away by customers for his more expert knowledge of wrenches, fittings, picks, and screws. In time, a cold, metallic scent seemed to her to cling to his clothes and flesh.

After hours, in the dim apartment behind the darkened shop, they took their evening meal, almost silent, their chief music the dull chime of tin forks on earthen plates and the crash of a pot lid. Table cleared, Klein tallied the day's receipts, then stored them, mouse quiet, in the vault of a steel strongbox deep in a recessed corner of his clothes closet. For half an hour he read the evening paper, snapping the tabloid pages in crisp, sharp folds as he turned them. Once or twice, he might comment aloud on the behavior of men and nations, his lips twisted with the sour humor of a scoffer whose worst expectations are fulfilled. Jennie, at her needle, would half-glance across the room in mechanical confirmation that no response was called for.

To bed at ten. Jennie coming from the bathroom, hair down and heavy with nightdress, to find Klein, in long underwear, winding the clock in swift ratchet movement and rasp of gears. Ice-blue walls paled by the sole bare bulb of the ceiling fixture dusted slowly toward zinc. The one window burglar barred. A three-piece suite of rock maple with bed stark in stiff folds of white linen. Here, Klein and Jennie lay in the parallel slumber of their wedlock, rest broken only by brief and intermittent coupling. Wordless then, even the surges of breath muffled beneath the sound of sheets crackling like chill foil.

Somber, severe, the Kleins' existence was nonetheless marked by the small virtues of steady income and fixed routine. Until the crash. Sales fell, profits contracted then disappeared, the supply of cash for mere subsistence dwindled. Torn between grim hope and despair, Klein either kept the store open long past its usual closing time on the chance of attracting an extra customer or two, or opened late, convinced that there was no trade to be had. With the petty precision of his days now gone, he led his life awry, like a failing clockworks—now too slow, too fast, too slack, too tightly coiled, then sprung at last to full halt, the moment marking in paradoxical exactness the onset of his long immobility. As legal notices were tacked to the door, Klein felt the blows as a sledge-hammer striking hard upon his stone gaze, and while there was no cry of pain, his vision was forever fractured.

Jennie took over. She had, perhaps, been more liberated than devastated by the loss. And, of course, there were two little ones to feed. Their father, she knew, would not provide. So leaving Klein and the children at opposite ends of the dark and airless fourth-floor walkup to which they had moved, she sought out relatives, beseeched charities, and haunted welfare agencies for their sustenance. She succeeded; they survived.

To Klein she said almost nothing. During an especially bad time or if she had to make her rounds in rough weather, she might admonish him obliquely:

"Now play quiet while I'm out, children, and don't bother your father, the goylem."

Once, struggling in the doorway with two bags of groceries and seeing Klein staring motionless at her through the gloom, she had called out:

"If your heart is a rock, must your hands and feet be cement?"

Klein did not reply, but putting aside the paper he had been reading by failing alley light, he rose, moved heavily toward her, and after placing one of the bags on the kitchen table, resumed his seat.

Jennie did not hate. She pitied, held him in contempt. In her sight, Klein was now less a rough equal than a dependent, a wayward child for whose welfare she was solely responsible. She advised him on scarves and sweaters, collars open or closed, sleeves rolled up or down; she spoke much on the price of bulbs and electricity as against the cost of blindness; she chose his diet. And her attitude pervaded not only the household but seeped through louring walls to their small world beyond.

"Does he take gravy with the potatoes?" her sister might ask Jennie at a rare family dinner, standing at Klein's chair as she spoke.

"Is it too hot for him in here?" her brother-in-law, all innocence, might wonder aloud as they sat in the living room hours later.

"Gravy gives him gas," Jennie would observe; or, "For him it's never cold enough."

Klein was silent.

But in the sixth year of decline, out of her own weariness and the hint of new times, Jennie spoke.

"Narducci, the fence place on Gerhardt Street, is hiring. I made you an eight-thirty appointment."

As if he had been waiting these long years just for her word, Klein appeared at Narducci Wire and Supply the next morning and was hired for both his physical strength and his knowledge of hardware. As a rule, he hated the work. The sun offended him and construction, even of fences, was unsettling. But the dead heft of the tools, the dull indifference of the materials were familiar, if not comforting. He liked barbed wire best, at times pausing to rub his calloused fingers over the twisting tips of the barbs, almost caressing them. So much the better if he drew blood. "Bastards," he would mutter then through taut lips, his steely eyes glinting in admiration.

He stayed two years then took to hauling for Boulevard Scrap Metal. It was, in part, a matter of more pay and shorter hours; in part, less constant labor; in part, in fine, a matter of intrinsic appeal. After dumping a load of his own or even during his lunch break, watching others unload, Klein would wander among the debris, king, if not of the mountain, then of the scrap heap. There were tales here of cracked tubs, rusted I-beams, mangled automobiles, whose plot lines he might surmise but whose endings he knew exactly.

"What'd you bring in today?" his boy would ask. (In the earliest days he sometimes spoke with his son.)

"Today? A Packard. Gray. Leather seats. Radio, lighter, and all. Crushed like a tin can.

His clenched fist trembled with excitement and strain.

"Some bigshot's car. Big deal. Look at it now."

His laugh, stifled through nose and teeth, sounded a low hiss, while beads of thin spittle welled in the corners of his mouth and wet his lips.

Then came the war. He was first on an assembly line producing shells, then in the manufacture of explosives, working his way up to deputy inspector. Klein was exact and thorough. Invariably, batches that he had pulled off the line proved defective.

He had more money now, did better than just get by. He replaced his ancient, pre-crash suit, grudgingly raised Jennie's household allowance as prices rose, and hoarded the rest. The children were Jennie's business.

What he could touch were the extra coins as he stood hands in pockets during leisure moments, rubbing them with his calloused fingers or tossing them together in muffled cacophonous jingle. Some evenings, he would empty them upon the kitchen table and arrange them in piles by denomination, only to sweep them noisily aside and begin again. The scent of iron and steel, that had clung to Klein all his adult days, was now seasoned with nickel, silver, and lead, and, though by purest coincidence, his hair turned almost at once a dark, metallic gray.

But early in '47 the plant closed and Klein was turned out. For three months he took to sitting at the window and reading newspapers as he had during the long years of depression. Jennie brooded—no matter that the scene had changed—a two-bedroom apartment on the second floor of a six-story elevatored building—the action, inaction, was the same. Then one day he was not at the window, and the next morning he left before Jennie was awake. Later, discovering that his old black lunch box was missing from the cupboard shelf, she sighed her relief without smiling and continued her chores.

From then until the year before his death, Leybele Klein worked for Rutland Demolition and Wrecking Company, first as a gang foreman, later, older then, as overseer of inventory and supply. He took to the job with eager efficiency, as a predator to prey. For the first time he felt his labors were complete. It was no longer a matter of selling a crowbar or presiding over a random heap piled largely by others, as at Boulevard Scrap. Now, he saw it all through from beginning to end, selecting the equipment and explosives, directing their use, distributing battered concrete, staved wood, or twisted metal to appropriate piles for subsequent crushing, shredding, or smelting. Even behind a desk in his last years he sensed the coherence, perhaps the more deeply because of his more accurate control and detachment from the actual events for which he was both strategist and compiler. Yet it was not pride in accomplishment that he felt, but the inevitability of process, precise and thorough dissolution. The corrosive pit of his being devoured all achievement, even his own, insatiable.

Klein shared nothing of this with Jennie, would not have had he known it himself. To her he gave part of his paycheck, the amount adjusted reluctantly as prices rose. He neither prospered nor starved. His small savings grew slowly. Belatedly, at Jennie's prolonged insistence, he broke down and bought a television set, a floor sample of a discontinued model. Yet, had he earned more, spent more, he would not have regained what he had lost, what, as he put it, had been taken from him years ago. Goal? Aspiration? He could not have said. For Klein, the prime article of faith had long been an abstract "they" wrongfully possessing a definite "mine."

If he had purpose at all, it was not in recovering the loss but in wreaking "I" upon "them" and "theirs." In such pronominal perception, all other distinctions were blurred. "You" also was "they" and "we" unrecognized.

Focused on such struggle, Klein did not look within. He was not well, but months passed before his symptoms urged themselves upon him. Prolonged stoppage, then sudden loosening of the bowels, then blood, then pain.

"Cancer," Jennie informed her children "Six months, maybe a year. His insides, they're rusting away."

Having numbered the virtues of Klein spouse, the funeral director's nephew cleared his throat, as if bits and pieces of his fabrication had lodged there. None of his auditors had perceived the subject through the veil, but most had gazed on hypnotically, content to be aware only of the honeyed gauze of the eulogy. Jennie wept a slow, thin stream of quiet tears—she could not have said why. The son and daughter, perhaps suppressing derisive laughter or controlling disdainful smiles, sat stone-faced in pro forma, if unwitting, tribute. More fitting still, Klein's only brother had declined to renew acquaintance after twenty years.

Throat cleared and moistened with genteel sips of water, the nephew of the funeral director resumed his fable—this time of Klein father—in which the words "care," "help," "encourage," "pride" and variants were prominent. Though seated on either side of their mother and spaced several feet apart along the mourners' bench, Harold Klein and his sister Doris reacted in unison, their bodies growing ever tense, their jaws rigid.

Leybele Klein had touched his offspring at arm's length, if at all, had never shared their games, had given them neither toys nor time. If his reply to their questions was not "go ask your mother," it was a stock response edged with sarcasm. The answer to all arithmetic questions was "twenty-two," to history questions, "George Washington." If shown a test or a report card, Klein would read the results without comment; he gave no advice about courses or careers. He was surprised rather than pleased when Harold received his B.S. in accounting from the city college. When Doris completed her two years at business school, he was merely relieved that his small contribution toward tuition had ceased. Klein attended both graduations as a captive of circumstance.

By then, however, the younger Kleins had long learned to avoid their father. Walking toward him, they circled slightly in passing or pressed their backs involuntarily to the wall and sidled on, as if fearful of encounter with a menacing stranger. If addressed, they spoke a few reluctant syllables in meager reply.

Reflecting on their childhood as the service droned on, each saw Klein as a blurred, malevolent mass huddled at the window late in a cold, dark winter afternoon, eyes wounding them like black needles if they raised their voices, but no sound from him, except for folded pages of the tabloid snapped sharply from the wrists, like a whip.

He did not beat them but deprived, denied, gave only bread and water for the soul. Six weeks in advance, knowing it would take a month's repetition to extract the needed money, Jennie would begin her semi-annual plea.

"It's getting to holiday. Harry needs a new suit."

"He got a suit last holiday."

"Not last holiday. A year ago already."

"So?"

"It doesn't fit, so. Four inches he grew this year."

"Sure, he eats like a horse."

Klein glared at the birdlike child looking on with large, sorrowful eyes from the doorway.

"Yeah, a horse," Jennie went on. "Two bites for supper. Maybe he gained three pounds this year."

"The cod liver oil. That's why he grows so much. Don't give it no more, so he'll grow normal and won't need clothes every Monday and Thursday."

"There's a sale soon by Shenkman."

"All right. All right. But the shoes take to stretch and the boy can polish himself."

"Nu," Jennie shrugged her acquiescence.

In the doorway, Harold Klein curled his crowded toes and rubbed one scuffed shoe against the other.

"Doris could also use . . ." Jennie began again.

"Don't give me Doris. I remember the green dress last spring, and so fast she's not growing."

"It's torn."

"There's no needles in the house?"

"A big hole."

"Put a patch."

"Who has material to match?"

"So it won't match. As long as she's not naked. And where did she get such a big hole?"

"Someone pushed her off the swing."

"I told you to tell her stay out of the park."

"A kid is a kid."

"Patch it."

Jennie thought a moment. With some contrasting fabric she could put two patch pockets on the dress and cover the hole.

"But shoes she must have."

Klein gauged her resolve.

"Get them a size big."

Weeks afterward, Klein took some bills from his cache in the old strongbox and laid them on the table. Jennie counted them, calculating expenses all the while.

Not another penny," Klein warned as she looked up.

Jennie said nothing as she thrust the bills into her purse. It was all right. This time she could make it.

Later on it was the same.

"That's a new record you're playing ten times? You just got one last week."

"It's just the other side."

"You'll wear it out with the Victrola together."

"Oh, Pop," Doris muttered between clenched teeth.

"That reminds me. You don't have to brush your hair in the mirror half an hour with the electric on. Who you farputsing for with lipstick, the boys already? You keep them away. I don't need no fifteen-year-old bomerke in the house."

"Mama!" she shrieked, and in tearful flight down the hall, "He's starting again!"

Oblivious to her, Klein called to Harold in the next room.

"That ball game still blasting?"

"It's a double header, Pop. two games."

"Two! I'll send the electric bill to Joe DiMaggio."

"Oh, Pop. A radio uses next to nothing."

"From all these next to nothings comes a lot of somethings."

"Yeah, especially if it goes extra innings," Harold dared.

"Don't be a wise guy, or off it goes altogether."

Later, with the younger Kleins married and raising families of their own, active fires of hostility were banked and cooled to a glacial indifference that extended to the third generation as well.

"Say hello to your grandfather, and give Grandma a kiss."

"Hello, Grandfather," the little ones murmured, turning toward Klein with eyes averted.

"Hello, hello," Klein grunted, twice flicking the back of a hand in their direction without looking up from his paper.

Duty done, they dashed away to Jennie.

"Hiya Grandma!!"

"The tummlers are here already, "Klein grumbled.

"What's new in the paper, Pop."

"What can be new? There's still only two kinds in the world, savages and shlemiels."

Harold's eyes met Klein's for an instant.

"That doesn't leave much room for maneuvering"

"No room for maneuvering, he says. Some accountant."

"When's Doris getting here?"

"She's not."

"Why? She said she'd come."

Harold's voice fell to near childish whine at having to deal with Klein alone.

"Why? Her husband, Mr. Delicate, is sick."

"Sick? When I spoke to him the other night, he was fine."

"Who knows? Cold feet, maybe," Klein replied, lips in sardonic half twist.

Speaking through his disappointment, and thinking of his absent wife as well, Harold replied with unusual candor.

"No one likes to be bullied, Pop. So he's a piano tuner. He makes a living, doesn't he? He hasn't asked you for a handout."

"That'll be the day."

"You said it."

"Go help." Klein jerked his head toward the kitchen.

More in despair than obedience, Harold sought out his mother and sons. Once, watching the boys in furtive play, he winced at the double image of his own childhood.

"Supper's ready," Jennie called minutes later.

"Give them. I'll eat myself," Klein replied.

Harold glanced toward his father, now shrouded in gray twilight, lamp within reach unlit. He swallowed hard, the persistence of pattern and memory stuck in the craw of his soul.

". . . remembered for good not only by family but by friends, neighbors, the community, and his people . . .," the director's nephew intoned.

Almost by turns, Jennie, Doris, and Harold glanced swiftly about the chapel, then more swiftly still, returned gaze front. Jennie was calm now, small weeping ceased, sufficient to ease a lifetime's festering.

There had been no friends—ever. Neighbors, only by proximity. One of them, for seventeen years Jennie's confidant, sat in the rear of the chapel—for Jennie's sake alone. Klein's hostility toward her had been no greater than toward others, though more than others she had exposed herself to it by intrusion upon his existence. He never answered her knock, never greeted her when she entered, never took notice of what she said, and always excluded her from any remark he might chance to make.

She was perhaps more fortunate than those whose apartments adjoined his, since Klein regularly chastised them for their offenses against him by beating a broom handle upon ceilings, floors and walls. If, at the New Year, two or three of the building's more forgiving residents offered a holiday greeting, Klein responded with an abrupt nod, as much rebuff as acknowledgement. Generally, he held both these and others in collective contempt, refusing, for instance, to join in their occasional legal squabbles with the landlord and forbidding Jennie to participate.

He had as little sympathy for their joy as for their troubles, refusing, for instance, to contribute to the block party after V-J Day and, despite the heat, shutting his window to the din.

In the world beyond his own four walls and those of the building, Klein maintained similar distance. He had never joined a labor union, let alone a social or civic club. During the depths of the depression, he had relinquished the burial society membership given him by his father, retaining the five-dollar annual dues for more immediate uses. "Real estate I can't afford," he had told the treasurer, ending a two-minute talk in the hallway.

He entered the synagogue around the corner twice a year at Jennie's urging, customarily enraged at the price of holiday tickets. No recourse here, but when the Hebrew school went to two dollars a week, he withdrew Harold and placed him in the hands of a private tutor at nearly half the rate, since Jennie again insisted that the boy receive some Jewish education. For Klein, the synagogue was populated by three alien types—snuff smellers, thieves, and cutthroats, with the rabbi and president serving as head crook and chief assassin, respectively. Theft and murder, though unspecified, offended his moral sense, and using snuff was a filthy habit, repugnant to the meticulous Klein, whose clothes were well-starched or ironed and whose hands, calluses aside, seldom bore traces of his rugged labor.

There were no donations.

"More than for tickets they won't get," he insisted. And the pronoun applied not only to the synagogue but to other causes as well. After Harold was removed from the school, the Jewish National Fund saw no more of Klein's nickels, though Jennie kept a secret charity box for the aid of widows and orphans.

In life, as in death, Klein had been all but alone. And while the coffin of the flesh had not assured the seclusion of the wooden one in which it now lay, he had managed, from time to time, to beat off the worms and vultures of his days and had licked the wound of his separateness free of their taint. At such moments, his bitter isolation might sweeten toward solitude and then, paradoxically, he was most at one with his kind.

On Sabbath afternoons, for instance, if he had not worked that day, or, in the long days of summer, whether he had worked or not, Klein would sit in half-dream at his window, newspaper folded on the floor, allowing the sun to warm him. Coiled still, reptilian, to be sure—but (children out at play and Jennie sitting with neighbors in front of the apartment building) the core of being itself now molten at the edges—lung, throat, lips tempered with the heat, would tremble first into living hum and then to song. Sweet—not as honey or fruit—but sweet as sea winds, or hay, or fresh water—thinly aflow from a rock no smiting could make yield. And in the ancestral tongue.

Neshome ru—peace for the soul—he began, both longing for it and lamenting its absence. Emotions—not necessarily his own—relieved only in the livelier refrain that spoke of his spirit's renewal in the Edenic emanations of each Sabbath.

Then, oddly for him—perhaps in response to unperceived regret, more inclusive.

Neshome ru—something his wife and children also lacked. Like someone blind, his lyric went on, the entire family saw life as eternally gray. Except again, for the weekly restoration.

Then, odder still, an unlikely expression of unity with his people.

Neshome ru—an offer of hope that his fellow Jews would achieve it and rejoice together in one eternal Sabbath.

And on repeatedly into early evening—or the click of a key in the lock, or a sash raised across the courtyard, or the coyote calls of derisive imitation from the boys at play in the alley below. Then, either at exposure or its threat, sudden silence, frost, and petrifaction.

Once, Klein had heard a boy admonish the others.

"Let him sing. He ain't half bad."

But it was too late. Klein had shut down.

"Yeah, he's all bad," came the stock rejoinder.

He had heard neither this nor the ensuing laughter at all.

It was over. The twenty-minute service to do earthly justice to Leybele Klein too long by eighteen. Guided by four black-suited attendants, the coffin was wheeled out a side door toward the hearse. The funeral director's nephew followed, intoning a hymn off key. The family followed him, expressionless. The few others dispersed.

Moments later, the hearse and one limousine, headlights on, began their slow journey toward the cemetery. No other car followed. Several times along its hour's route, the meager procession was an object of ridicule and jest. That evening, as they would for seven days, the family of Leybele Klein sat on low stools in hollow mourning.

Half a continent away, on a higher stool in a small cafe in a college town, a balding entertainer in jeans and open-collared plaid shirt talked to the sparse and inattentive crowd as he tuned a guitar.

"The next one I'd like to do—set up there D string—is a song I learned from an old guy we used to give fits when I was a kid. Mean sonofabitch—deserved it too. But he could sing—when he sang—about every three weeks or so. He didn't teach it to me. I kinda overheard it. If heeda known I was listenin', he woulda stopped. Told you he was a sonofabitch.

"Anyway, he sang it in another language and about one bunch of folks. But I figure it applies to one and all. (Down a little now D string.) Old man Klein. Taught it to my two-year-old the other week. 'Sing Oma' Kein', Daddy," she says. 'Oma' Kein' song.' Misses a few sounds now and then. Hope you won't. D string's sittin' just fine."

He played a brief upbeat arpeggio, and in the American mélange of country, folk, blues, and rock, began:

Restin' easy brother in my soul—
Restin' easy brother in my soul—
On the day I find a little peace of mnd,
I'll be restin' easy brother in my soul. . .

At the end there was scattered applause from the near empty house and a few whistles of approval. The singer acknowledged them.

"I thank you. Old Man Klein thanks you, too, wherever he is. I'm just sayin' that. Probably wouldn't. Me-ean!"

His few listeners murmured something verging on voiceless

laughter and breathed smiles. He resumed his patter.

"Meanest thing in the world—next to Klein—is a set of strings from the five and dime. These were the five. . .

The heavenly court had assembled to sit in Klein's judgment.

"His song," the defense had argued, "his song shows that he did not break the bonds altogether. A fact, regardless of intent," he added, anticipating the prosecution. "And who, even among us, can judge intent? Perhaps the song was the one cry he could still make. Why else sing at an open window in the midst of day? And the bond has now passed beyond the next generation to the one after that, beyond one's lawful obligation. The voice is still heard even should the name be lost. If not vindication, does this not call for mercy, mercy at least?"

The prosecutor had smiled throughout the hyperbole. He knew the case was his. Having presented no argument himself, he called now for the weighing of deeds. With the charity born of confidence, he permitted the song and its legacy to be placed first in the pan of righteousness. For a moment, the balance tipped benevolently, a fleeting testament to the possibility of Klein's virtue; and then the other deeds in the second pan and reversal, all but complete.

"Condemned," the jurors chorused mournfully.

There was silence, but the defender rose, duty laden, to plead before sentencing.

"I cannot quarrel with the wisdom of this court," he began, head bowed. "The life has been weighed and judged, according to divine law and to all earthly appearances, rightly. Indeed, it is out of full respect for the wisdom of the court that I now speak. Undeniably, the injury inflicted by this soul upon others is greater than his cry for reunion with the race from which he stood willfully apart. Undeniably, the small virtue of his song did not relieve wife and children of his burden nor preserve more total strangers against his chill hostility. Undeniably, it failed, at last, to save him.

"But equally undeniably," he looked up, "the one worthy act has spared—us—narrowly—from a new ignominy. As once we were accused of permitting self-denial to the point of abject submission to all evil, so without the slight merit in question here we might have been charged with tolerating, perhaps with producing, unmitigated ill. The soul of Leybele Klein has been judged, and justly, irredeemable, yet, has it not redeemed redemption itself?"

He sat heavily. The prosecutor had stopped smiling. Beneath the defender's rhetoric lay a truth, which stabbed, if not to the hallowed heart, then toward some other sainted spot. At least, it had touched the unhealed wound of that earlier case, reminding the otherwise perfect assembly once again of its own possible excess and liability.

Amid the sober hush, the judge spoke in slow soft syllables confirming the verdict.

"Condemned . . .

And then softer still, in tremulous whisper more thankful than forgiving, perhaps ashamed that no more could be said—

. . . but not utterly."

Concluding Service

Late Yom Kippur afternoon, rather later than usual, Abraham Shulman opened the ark to reveal the sacred scrolls and begin the Concluding Service. This honor had been his both by purchase and custom for nearly thirty years—at first because his donations to Beth Am had been generous and frequent and, later, also out of reverence for his advanced age. Now, well into his eighties, he stood to one side of the ark and listened as the cantor intoned the first solemn prayer.

"Too quick," he thought. "What's the rush?" Shulman's unpleasant observation passed momentarily as he looked out over the congregation—his congregation—all standing now, numbers swollen with the High Holiday overflow. He smiled benevolently, but as he glimpsed Emmanuel Garfein leaning hard upon his walker at the rear, his smile dissolved in the sobering gust of a sigh. He did not notice the young bloods—those who would slip out to catch an hour or two of the World Series or a football game—as they joked in whispers below him.

"Think he'll make it this year?" asked one, indicating Shulman with his head.

"Why not," said another, "he's been in training since July."

For nearly a decade now the Yom Kippur congregants had been impressed by the old man's ability to remain standing for the whole of the hour-long service. And every year at its conclusion he had made a circuit of the sanctuary, beaming as he accepted congratulations on his endurance and wishes for his continued strength—"Yasher koakh," or "A fine job Mr. Shulman," depending on the age and background of his greeter—and even jesting accusations that he'd eaten that day.

"I'll give three to one against him," said a third.

"Three to one, what?"

"Pieces of herring."

The would-be gambler was poked into submissive silence for reminding his peers of food in this twenty-fifth hour of their fast.

By now, Shulman had turned to face the ark. He shook his head once more as the cantor quickened his pace but soon lapsed into reverie. Over the years, Shulman had felt a growing need for this annual hour of reflection. Thumbing through the Book of Life before it's sealed he called it—only half in jest, his pragmatic face grinning embarrassment at such unproductive and superstitious contemplation. He knew, of course, that it was the physical trial that mattered.

It had not been so bad a life. "From remnants to riches," Shulman often joked. There had been struggle but no poverty. Marriage. Children. Ownership of a textile business. And with wartime profiteering, more than comfortable wealth. "Who didn't do it?" he shrugged mentally. "Besides, I had my losses too." He glanced left and right at the memorial windows for the son killed at Normandy and the wife who could not bear the shock, brushing in turn a thumb and forefinger across the pouches beneath his eyes.

Shulman had come to Nassatogue several years after the war, bringing his daughter and her family with him to a custom-built house on a two-acre plot. There was a three-room suite with bath and private entrance for him. He paid the mortgage and played, occasionally, with his grandchildren. His daughter kept house. Otherwise, he and his family lived the separate lives of considerate neighbors.

"Altogether, not a bad idea." Shulman thought.

In his early fifties, he was already in semi-retirement, visiting his office twice a week or so and making seasonal trips to the mill. Once, he had stayed on for more than a month to supervise the final conversion from silk to synthetics. With time and money to spare, Shulman turned to the construction of Beth Am—not as an act of faith, nor as response to a felt communal need, but as an exercise of the powers which had brought him success, lest they diminish with disuse: physical stamina, mental vigor, and the persistence to push an intangible idea to its tangible fulfillment. "Look, Manny," he had said when his pious friend Garfein cautioned against overexertion, "We'll go partners. You do the prayers; I'll do the heavy lifting."

He had served on the building and rabbi selection committees and had headed the fund-raising drive. "The arms I twisted still got the bruises," he thought. His hand reached involuntarily toward his heart, upon which throughout the day he had told his sins with clenched fist and unusual rigor.

The founding had cost two years of his time, much sleep, and a year's income. But he had laid the cornerstone himself and had seen personally both to the installation of the memorial windows and the construction of the religious school that bore his name. Not least, he had been chosen for a three-year term as president—by acclamation. The office had required his regular attendance at services and ex-officio membership on various committees. But his absences, selective but not infrequent, had been little noticed.

For a brief moment, Shulman was drawn from his reflection. The hum of the cantor's rapid chanting had given way to an operatic peroration. And now the new rabbi (he had served eleven years) stepped forward with an announcement: "We continue with the service on page 421." Shulman blanched.

"Three pages. That's a good five minutes they're leaving out. As if the service in the new makhzor isn't short enough already. Always changes. Everything changes," he thought. For an instant he allowed his erect bearing to slump into the posture of age. Then, righting himself, but with mood unaltered, he lapsed into tranquility once more.

There had been a second term as president—by election this time, but beyond that he would not run. "It's like cards," he had explained to Manny and their pinochle companion Meyer Kaminsky. "You quit while you're ahead." New and sometimes more money was coming into the congregation and always younger men. On leaving office, he was honored with a three-hundred-dollar a plate dinner (proceeds to the school fund) and with the unveiling of a presidential tablet bearing his name and dates of tenure. The plaque left ample room for those to follow.

He was in his sixties then, reluctant to accept a place among the gray-heads of the congregation and too restless and realistic to make much of the hollow title of Past President. While his donations to Beth Am remained as ample as ever, he was rarely seen on the premises. He was still active in the business, but his life centered increasingly on matters closer to home. There were his grandchildren's educations to be paid for. "Not that you can't, Phil," he had told his son-in-law, "but that I want." Phil hadn't argued, accepting Shulman's willfulness with the amused tolerance of a near equal, for the financial gap between them had narrowed. Later, after young Brian was caught with pills, there were legal and medical fees to be paid.

Brian's trouble had bewildered him. "Where's the profit in it? Where's the profit?" Shulman would repeat half shouting, half pleading to Manny. "The boy got everything he wants!"

"From too much you can also be meshuge," Manny would answer slowly, sadly. It was his friend's tone that soothed Shulman, as if the wisdom of the ages spoke through that tired, sickly body.

He had known Emmanuel Garfein years ago when they were young men traveling the same territory for rival companies. "The scholar" he was called then. Not that Manny wouldn't take a hand or two on the way to Boston. But he was that rare salesman who read something besides the Daily News.

"Oh, a two-book trip," Shulman sometimes teased, discomfort tempered by admiration, "one coming, one going." He patted his sample case. "Me too. Orders and accounts."

Manny did not last. He drifted into a small retail dry goods business specializing in seconds. For thirty-five years and with occasional stretching he made ends meet until persuaded by failing health and declining receipts to give it up and move in with his daughter. He had a room behind the kitchen and his books— no longer fiction but sacred texts.

Garfein had come to Nassatogue at the start of Shulman's first term. With a neighborhood, living arrangements, an interest in the synagogue at least partly in common, and with old times to talk over besides, the pair renewed their acquaintance. Once Shulman left office, they fell increasingly together, and in their reticent sharing of troubles great and small and in their equally brief mutual commiseration, the bond between them tightened toward friendship.

Two or three afternoons a week they met in Shulman's rooms, joined by Kaminsky, a retired pharmacist.

"Our 'professional' man, we called him," Shulman mused. The half-mocking title was his and Manny's small revenge on the druggist for his equally humorous and detached attitude toward both Garfein's observance and Shulman's earnest practicality.

"For prescriptions you must have charged by the word," Shulman often said, attempting to resume a game that Kaminsky had interrupted with one of his interminable anecdotes.

"So, anyway, I told her," Kaminsky might have concluded, "Lady, if you want your Sammy to take it, instead of chocolate in the malted put the Ex-Lax." Then turning to Shulman: "And don't be such a knaker—a big shot. What kind of game would you have without me?"

"What kind of game do we have with you?" Shulman would rejoin.

"Sha! Sha!" Manny the peacemaker would chime in. "Right is right."

Shulman would nod his reluctant agreement. "Yeh. Three-handed is better than nothing. And could you find a fourth in such a place on a Tuesday afternoon?"

"And if you could," Kaminsky might have continued, mending the momentary rift, "what would he play? Poker? Bridge?"

"Canasta?" Manny might have added.

"Everything they call a game," Shulman would observe. "Who deals?"

Play would continue with three dissonant sighs, the cards lifted like ancient and familiar burdens.

Sometimes, perhaps once a month, the three traveled to a Russian bath on the lower East Side. Afterward, they would eat at Ratner's, where Manny would invariably leave the tip while Shulman and Kaminsky quarreled over the check. At Ratner's, Kaminsky would assault the waiter:

"Is this a dairy restaurant? So how come you got a thumb in my soup?"

And the stock rejoinder:

"You want I should serve with dirty hands?"

"Such a Kaminsky!" Shulman thought. He remembered a time at the community center, just before Passover, when the druggist had scattered crystals of pharmaceutical dye about the swimming pool, staining patches of water a brief but bloody red, terrifying the bathers, then delivering half a mock sermon on the plagues of Egypt before being ushered out.

"Kaminsky," Shulman shrugged. He recalled standing at his bedside after the heart attack. "Nu?" he had asked with tender gruffness. "A sheyner gelekhter," Kaminsky had managed in a hoarse, ironic gasp through a pained half smile. Hardly "a fine joke." Two days later he was dead.

"Seven, eight years he's gone," thought Shulman, attempting to sharpen the blurred edges of the fading past. In his mournful struggle he barely heard the cantor's second crescendo and missed the rabbi's announcement of the page altogether. Nor was he aware that the memorial windows were now illuminated more fully by the lights of the sanctuary than by the rapidly setting sun.

The card games and monthly outings had both ceased with Kaminsky's death. And shortly thereafter he had gone into full retirement, selling all but twenty percent of his interest to the junior partner he had taken on years earlier. Now, he was the "junior" partner and a silent one at that. "If Phil only came into the business . . . But he did all right for himself in appliances. Three stores. And the grandchildren—a dentist, a librarian—they'll have an interest? And Brian, who knows—even with the real estate— what's gonna be with him yet? If not for the war . . . If Marcus. . . If, if . . . What's the use?"

Weariness and boredom had prompted his decision in part, but really, once Edna was gone it had seemed increasingly pointless to make the trip to the city. He had met her a year or two after Lillian's death. She was an assistant bookkeeper for a Seventh Avenue dress house, a war widow, not yet thirty, childless. What began as casual sympathy grew slowly toward a clandestine May-December romance, whose moderate passion belied the intensity of caring. "Let's call it June-October," she had kidded him at moments when Shulman brooded about the twenty-odd years between them. Perhaps because he attached too much importance to their ages, because he was reluctant to ripple the placid waters of family relationships, because she made no demands, because there seemed to be no need, they had not married. His moving to Nassatogue had confirmed, not established the understanding between them.

Shulman's occasional weekends away or nights spent in the city might have aroused suspicions, but Phil and Bea said nothing. And in a sense the possibility was beyond his daughter's comprehension. "When Pop looks at a skirt," she had often told Phil, "it's to inspect the fabric." Phil would nod in agreement, perhaps keeping his own silent counsel. Shulman himself told no one—certainly not Kaminsky, who would have ridiculed—not Manny, who, uncomfortable and abashed, would have shrugged.

Edna had been a corner of his life apart—his refuge, retreat, the source of sporadic rejuvenation. As for her, care and caring were the sap that sustained the willow of her being past a fading and disappointed youth and preserved it against the blight of brittle widowhood. Shulman had not kept her. "You won't take, and I won't ask," he once told her. "And better you should pay your own rent and eat your own bread." But the luxuries were his—the weekends, the dinners out, a piece of jewelry now and then, a small fur, a pair of season's tickets to the opera. "Take a friend," he had said. "I can't listen to that."

He fingered the band of the gold watch she had given him for a birthday present one year. "So you know when it's time to leave," she had smiled sadly. The reproach had not been fair, though it was true that by then he rarely stayed the night. Even his two-day-a-week work schedule had become taxing, and he was embarrassed when on evenings after dinner he fell asleep for an hour or two on Edna's sofa. "Fine company I am," he would yawn sheepishly on awakening. It was more than sleeping that he meant. Of late, his sexual powers had been failing. Interest was sporadic, arousal slow., and fumbling apologies a source of mutual discomfort. Most nights it was better to talk, watch TV or see a show, and then catch the late train to Nassatogue. What had once been romance had become increasingly quiet companionship.

"But," Shulman thought, "like Manny would say, a person is only flesh and blood. How long could things go on like that? Almost two years—who could expect more?" He had begun the separation—though not deliberately—by slowly withdrawing from her life. If Edna's comparative youth was not a threat, it was, at least, a challenge—a challenge that demanded more energy than he could usually summon to overcome the advancing inertia of his years.

Instead of twice a week, he saw her once. Instead of once a week, every other week or so—irregularly at last. He was prepared when she told him.

"How old is he?" he had asked.

A whisper.

"Fifty-six."

A wince and recovery.

"He likes opera?"

A nod.

"You can't beat that."

"They were good years, Abe," she had said, hoarse and tearful, at the door.

"The trouble is, Edna, that June-October becomes too soon September-January. Mazl tov."

He had patted her hand and kissed her forehead, ending it in sympathy just as it had begun.

Long months later she returned his wedding gift. A three-word note accompanied the check: "As ever, Edna." Shulman smiled and shook his head, acknowledging the futility of his gesture. He destroyed the draft and wrote another for the same amount to Beth Am, donating it as if in her honor.

A momentary pause in the chant and the rustling of pages being turned roused Shulman to near attention. He thumbed through the prayer book mechanically, print visible as shapes though unperceived and then sight itself blurring once more as the cantor resumed.

Beth Am. With Edna, the business, Kaminsky, and pinochle gone, he had become increasingly a part of it, at least as witness to its daily routine. Though never religious, he now attended morning minyen, with Manny, two or three other retired men and the rabbi, helping to form a reliable nucleus for the required ten. Mourners and those who had yortzeit could usually be counted on for the remainder. He would lead the service if pressed but preferred to sit reciting the prayers as he had in childhood—mumbled and uncomprehending. Afterward, there were bagels and coffee and half an hour's talk with the older men. Twice a week he attended the rabbi's study sessions, listening in desultory fashion to the wisdom expounded, asking a rare question or commenting if the subject turned to business. Otherwise, he would busy himself in the office, stuffing envelopes or answering the phone. Sometimes, he spent an hour or two in the library leafing through a pile of well-illustrated books while Manny sat opposite scanning a chapter of Talmud. In fine weather, the friends might sun themselves on the low brick wall bordering the lawn.

On occasional afternoons, Shulman would appear in a Hebrew School classroom. "Most of our children have no extended family nearby and many of them have very little regular contact with a senior adult," the education director had explained cheerfully. "You can be our resource person."

"You mean," he had said, "you want the kids should meet an old man."

But he did not mind spending half an hour telling how it was a lifetime ago in Williamsburg or half a life ago in Midwood. And lost in the telling, he was unaware of the incongruity of blank stares on bright faces. Still, the children were in awe of him—an alien being, yet somehow half familiar.

Shulman was known, then, throughout Beth Am's generations. His age, his omnipresence, the fact that he had been the principal founder and first president, and that he was a benefactor still, placed him beyond the bounds of common congregational humanity. He had become a fixture. "Like a chandelier," he had remarked this morning, in anticipation of his honor, "once a year they dust me off."

It was more difficult at home. He measured afternoons by the length of naps, the arrival of mail, and by when he might reasonably begin setting the table before his daughter and son-in-law returned from work. The mortgage had long been paid and the grandchildren, even Brian, were educated and gone. Except for the ceremonial gathering of the clan at Passover, Shulman, his small routine broken, was inclined to be put out by their visits. "Royalty's coming?" he would say to Bea on those Sunday mornings when she fussed about his cigar stubs in her living room ashtrays. And ten minutes of dandling his great-granddaughter Jennifer were enough. Phil and Bea themselves led prosperous, active middle lives of work and play. They were not inattentive, occasionally making themselves available for Sunday dinner out as Shulman's guests and frequently inviting him to join them on their vacations. He refused to accompany them.

"A cruise I'll take? In twenty years I didn't even take the Staten Island ferry. And what'll I do on the boat? Play tennis? Dance with the captain in a conga line? I can stay home and do nothing just as easy. Besides, here I have the shul and Manny."

Invariably, Bea would seize such moments to encourage his joining a "golden age" club. Invariably, grim, Shulman would reply: "A golden age I can't afford." Bea would throw up her hands, freeze two weeks' worth of meals, and ask Garfein's daughter to look in on him. At this, Shulman would bristle with genuine though half-suppressed anger. "If you gonna get me a—a baby sitter, she should be twenty-two and blond."

Later, maudlin and self-indulgent, he might commiserate with Manny, the two seated beside each other, a pair of ill-assorted peas in a common pod.

"You know what we are, Manny? Shmates. Remnants."

Garfein would hold up his trembling hand and smile feebly. "Seconds." And after a pause: "Me, I got one foot in the grave already."

And Shulman suddenly recovering himself: "Listen, like Kaminsky, may he rest in peace, used to say, better one foot in the grave than two feet in Long Beach."

Manny would nod his assent, grateful that he had so far avoided that sprawling undertaker's anteroom of old age and nursing homes.

"But Manny, Manny," Shulman sighed to himself, "we almost lost you. Two strokes in three years. And the second time fifty-fifty."

Garfein's illness had affected him deeply. He had known death—had lost a wife and son, Kaminsky—but not such dying—not time's slow erosion nor the piecemeal sundering of disease which sent the life in clattering fragments down and thrust it, precariously poised, toward the last avalanche of annihilation. It had frightened him at first, then angered him, much as an unethical, undercutting competitor might have. But here the offender was invisible, and though Shulman could not have expressed it, obscene.

He had striven mightily for Manny's life, the second time especially, sharing the necessary ministrations with Garfein's daughter and driving his friend beyond the limits of rehabilitation with which Manny himself might have been content. At times, he had gone well past encouragement to anxious insistence and rage. "You put one foot in front of the other. All your life you been doing it. You forgot how all of a sudden? Walk, goddammit! Walk!"

He had ignored Manny's tears and slow, weak, thick-tongued recriminations. And Garfein had walked. He could even take a few steps without support. But the half smile on Shulman's lips dissolved to reflective drooping at the corners of the mouth. "For what?" he thought. "To wait for the next one? Who knows?" But a standoff in such cases was a kind of victory, and Manny was far better off than others in similar circumstances might have been.

His own health was good and a source of confidence if not of pride. "But you never know," he sometimes worried in darker moments. "Some people are never sick a day and all of a sudden . . ." Then, he would shake himself, as he did now, and leave his thought implicitly clear but magically incomplete.

He might be stiff in the joints some mornings, and rich foods upset his stomach. But so much the better for his weight—though somehow his once robust build had gone more to bone than fat and each year his shirt collar hung more loosely about his hollow throat. In his prime, he had been above average height and seemed hardly to have shrunk beyond the barest stooping of the shoulders. His muscles, though wearied, had remained firm, the progress from chest to abdomen creating but the gentlest of slopes. While his legs had lost their former spring, and he could no longer move at the pace with which he had once bounded between shipping and showroom, he was agile enough to change an occasional fluorescent lamp in Beth Am's office, climbing up on a desk and reaching high overhead above the protests of the secretaries. For years he had taken a daily solitary walk, now shorter and less vigorous than in the days when Kaminsky had called him "Hershele Truman," but still even-paced and dignified.

"Well preserved," Shulman sneered silently, "—like a herring in a jar."

But more than the irregular displays of agility, more even than the ritual walk, it was this ceremony at the Concluding Service during the past decade that bore greatest witness to his endurance and sustained him. Reflection was cathartic, to be sure, but the sheer physical feat of standing for a full hour was crucial. "I have done it. I am renewed. I will survive." So his secret liturgy ran. It was as if by an act of will made manifest in the durable but declining flesh that Shulman hoped to have himself inscribed in the Book of Life for the coming year, oblivious for now to prayer, penitence, and charity, the conventional means of entry. And each year the awed acknowledgment of the congregation appeared to seal his success.

The young bloods were right. He had been in training for weeks. Preparation—he would have called it. Purification—he might have felt. One did not come casually to his annual confrontation with destiny. He had slept more, eaten more carefully, gradually lengthened his walks and elevated his legs twice a day to improve circulation. He had withdrawn, grown quiet, and taken to reading a brief daily portion of the High Holiday services. "Getting ready for your show, Pop?" Bea and Phil had teased as usual. Nor had Manny understood. "You remind me of my mother," he had said to Shulman once again. "She got so scared around the holidays she prayed twenty times a day."

"How do you tell someone? How do you explain?" Shulman thought. "Even if you could understand yourself."

He was interrupted by someone tugging at his sleeve and pointing with a prayer book. After a moment's daze, he understood and stepped forward to close the ark. "Yes, it's dark enough," he thought, looking toward the windows. But on checking his watch, Shulman realized that the service had taken just forty-three minutes. He studied the second hand. No, it hadn't stopped. How was it possible? Had so much been omitted? Had the cantor chanted so rapidly the little that was read?

Pale with resentment and dismay, Shulman touched the proffered hands of the rabbi and cantor and descended the bimah steps. The customary greetings, tinged with bitter humor to his ears, rang unavoidably above the hasty and hungry mumble of anticlimactic evening prayers.

"Nu, Reb Avrom, you did it again," someone boomed. "But this year," he teased, "they took it easy on you." No matter that like many of the congregants he had seated himself long ago.

"May you live out the year and do it again next Yom Kippur," another intoned familiarly. The blessing struck Shulman to the heart like an omen of doom.

Across the sanctuary, the herring gambler defended himself against his youthful peers.

"Look, when I said three to one, I meant for a whole service. Besides, none of you took the bet."

His protest was drowned in half-stifled catcalls and mock-derisive cries of "Welsher!" that dissolved into laughter at last.

Meanwhile, Shulman made his way along an outer aisle, eyes downcast, dismissing adulation with a shrug and avoiding as many greeters as possible. He did not make a circuit of the synagogue but paused at the rear to sit beside Manny.

"You know what, my physical therapist," Garfein confided, "not counting a few times I sat down two minutes, I stood up as long as you."

"A new competitor," Shulman muttered.

Then they were quiet. When the great blast of the shofar sounded, they shuffled out together and were swallowed up by the surging crowd.

A Judgment/An Appeal

At ease before the expanse of his library table, Rabbi Isaac Alter gazed through an oversized window across the mauve stubble of November plains, then turned to the lean visitor in tie and sober tweeds poised and expectant in the chair before him.

"I am flattered, of course, "Alter began, "but less flattered than surprised."

He attempted a smile and shifted his weight, as if embarrassed both for the frankness of his own response and the request that had prompted it.

"After all, he continued, "a young man such as yourself, in these times, and in such a place . . ."

He trailed off, gesturing toward the window with a fleshy hand.

"The point is," he resumed, "that young people today seem more inclined to rely upon themselves or upon resources not so . . . official . . . as myself."

"You are a rabbi," the young man replied, as much to verify as to state the fact.

"Yes, but a rather rare bird of a rabbi—a bachelor and a circuit rider—a kind of two-headed calf," Alter jested.

A smile twitched in polite response.

"Still, you are a rabbi."

"For two hundred miles around I am *the* rabbi. A pioneer, a frontiersman on the edge of Judaism, and a bit of a cowboy. Rounding up the strays you see. A shopkeeper in This-ville. A professional in That-burg. A bris here, a funeral there every few years, and once in a blue Yom Kippur a gathering of ten or twelve to hold a service at the U.

"Otherwise," he went on, speaking as much to himself as to his guest, "a lecture at the Rotary, a Fourth of July speech, an invited sermon every few years—all as de facto emissary to the gentiles—and once in a great while— now, for instance, counselor and sage."

Returning from the edge of reverie, Alter leaned back, arms folded beneath his paunch.

"So, tell me."

The young man gripped the arms of his chair and leaned forward.

"As I said, it concerns the young woman to whom I'm engaged. She too is Jewish."

"Too much surprise is not good for the heart," Alter interrupted, touching a hand to his chest.

The response was a puzzled stare.

"Forgive me. Please continue."

"We have known each other for two years and were engaged six months ago," his visitor resumed as if no interruption had occurred.

"My prospective bride has many excellent qualities. She is educated, handsome, talented—plays piano and often sews her own clothes; she likes children, cooks, and will have less difficulty than most in managing a household since she has good financial judgment and can do much of her professional work while at home.

"She is a charitable woman, honest, refined, and gracious. For these and a thousand other virtues I love her dearly."

"And your parents?"

"They too love her."

"Friends?"

"They adore her."

Then, reading Alter's bewilderment, he went on—more rapidly now, pitch raised.

"But you see, Rabbi, that is part of the problem. She is so—amiable. Friendly. Much too friendly."

"And you fear that while she is at home, working and managing the household, she might run off with the postman?"

"No, no. Not that exactly. But she is so indiscriminate that it irks me. For instance, when she's pleased with me, she'll peck me on the nose. But her cat or the wide-eyed six-year-old on the reservation is likely to provoke the same response."

He drew a deep, slow breath, then resumed obliquely.

"Rabbi, do you know Browning?"

Alter nodded right and left.

"My Last Duchess?"

Another nod.

"Well, she reminds me of her."

"The duchess was innocent."

"Yes. But to excess."

"A paradox. I haven't dealt with one since my yeshiva days," Alter laughed.

But observing the tight-lipped visage before him, he returned at once to more sober focus.

"Remember, young man, it was the duke whose behavior was excessive."

"He cannot be justified in any way. But to live with that provocation, that 'spot of joy' which should be yours alone called up for all alike. . ."

"To be shared?"

"Yes."

"Even innocently."

"Yes."

"You fear, then, that your fiancé is too gregarious."

"Yes."

"And that this blemish might obscure the thousand virtues named and unnamed alike."

"Yes."

"And, finally, because of this possibility you wish to know whether I think you should, in fact, marry her."

His visitor nodded decisively.

Alter stared at him, drumming his fingers on the table in arrhythmic reflection. The other, gaze averted, shuffled his cap from hand to hand with rapid pulse-like movements.

"I will tell you a story," Alter said at last.

The young man stiffened.

"If you have patience for Browning, a few minutes of Alter won't be so bad. Relax. Enjoy—at least until the moral.

"By the way, what is it you do?"

"Anthropology."

"Ah—a folktale then."

The caller shrugged his reluctant assent.

Then, staring out upon the barren plains once more, Alter began.

"Once in my father's town, a young man of excellent family, well respected himself, also a scholar, was engaged to a young woman of great beauty and flawless reputation, descended from rabbis on her mother's side and herself the daughter of the town's wealthiest inhabitant, a pious man. The match, as was the custom, had been arranged, but to the couple's great delight, for they had long known each other and loved secretly. A fairy tale.

"Their engagement announced, the couple met more freely—with family or friends present or alone—innocently, taking a Sabbath stroll beside the riverbank, talking of news from neighboring villages, sharing—discreetly— a secular Yiddish story or two. And they found that their families' approval brought increased devotion, that their secrecy had been an impediment to love, not its source.

"Idyllic, yes, but what paradise lacks a serpent?

"One evening the young woman's father gave a feast to celebrate the signing of the engagement contract. Escaping the din of merriment for a few minutes, the prospective groom made his winding way up the flight of steps to the quiet of the second story. Though he had visited before, he remained fascinated by the novelty and luxury of a two-story house and studied the intricate carving of the railing as he ascended, admired the quality of the hardwood floors and baseboards in the corridor above, felt with his eyes along the arabesques of deep-piled carpets.

"But as he came to the end of his sensuous journey, he noticed a flicker of light in the small sewing room beyond the bedrooms. Drawn mothlike, he approached the door, which stood open just a crack, and touched it softly with his fingertips. It moved on silent hinges three or four inches more.

"Within, a full-length mirror stood before him, imaging a spare cot and his betrothed who sat upon it. She hummed as she repaired the edge of her petticoat, now raised well above her knee.

"The young man turned away in his embarrassment, then turned back at once in his fascination. It was only her leg, the right, innocently exposed but immodest to look upon. He turned away again.

"Her humming at her work drew him back once more, and as he turned this time, he saw her reach behind her thigh just above the knee and rub indolently. He recalled how through her heavy dress she might sometimes touch that very spot. And now, her hand removed and flesh bared, he saw the black half-inch mole with its two or three stiff, bristling hairs. But in an instant, as she rose and turned to the mirror to adjust her clothes, petticoat and skirt fell into proper place. She smiled to herself; he withdrew in haste, sickened.

"For days the talk in synagogue and tavern was all of his taking ill at the feast. In the market place, old heads were shaken—a few in pity, more in fear—with comment divided generally between ominous prediction and ribald jest.

"Toward week's end, when he had left his bed for a chair in the main room, she came to visit. At first, his conversation was constrained, his voice feeble, but a half hour of her pleasant talk seemed to revive him. They were laughing together at the escapades of a friend when she passed an unconscious hand along her thigh. His laughter turned shrill; he grew pale; his palms sweaty.

" 'What is it?' She hurried toward him.

" 'Nothing. Don't touch me. Only a little fever. Stand back— some air.'

"She summoned his mother who helped him back to bed.

"But by the following Sabbath his recovery seemed more complete, and he attended services for the first time since falling ill. It was a pleasant April afternoon, and after the midday meal he felt well enough to accompany his betrothed on their now customary Sabbath walk. He had seen her at the synagogue smiling at him through the curtain that divided the women's section from the men's. He had smiled back.

But now, calling at her house, he felt uneasy, retreating half a step when she opened the door but entering as she left to retrieve her coat. Waiting, he followed the curve of the staircase to the floor above and in his mind's eye retraced his brief, unfortunate journey to the sewing room. When his fiancé returned, he was still shuddering.

" 'Perhaps we should stay indoors,' " she suggested quietly.

" No!' he snapped. 'We must go out. We must. I mean, the day is too fine to waste. The sunlight and air will restore me.'

" 'If you think so,' she agreed. But her voice was tight with concern.

"He opened the door for her, keeping it between them until she passed. Outside, he seemed to disappear from view.

"'Oh, there you are,' she laughed, discovering him at her left. 'I thought I'd lost you.'

"'No.'

" 'You always walk on the other side.'

" 'Habit, comfortable though it may be, is a great destroyer. Today I will see you from a new perspective and perceive a new truth.'

"His lips smiled but his eyes did not.

" 'And I you?'

" 'Perhaps. It depends on where you look—and why.'

"As he spoke, a bird in flight caught her eye. She followed its slow descent to the riverbank.

" 'The cranes are nesting.'

"He had turned away to study a bare sapling stunted beneath the spread of an oak in early leaf.

" 'There will be no nests this year.'

"Startled by his seeming denial, she turned toward him, questioning. He pointed to the dead tree.

" 'Oh, I see.'

"As she stood in momentary abstraction, her right hand brushed against her thigh. He saw the movement and cut it short.

" 'Let's walk.'

"His abruptness bordered on command.

 "They went on for a time in silence.

"Twice more during their walk he managed to distract her as she threatened to touch the offending spot, and by the end of the afternoon he knew her left profile thoroughly. Leaving her at her door at last, he returned home, triumphant in restraint. Alone in her room, the young woman lay crushed by the day's inexplicable tension. She wept, praying that his recovery might yet be perfected.

"For some weeks there seemed to be no change. But after the festival of Sh'vues—Shavuot—he spoke with her.

" 'I have been thinking—studying and thinking—thinking and studying. The result is that I believe that for two people not yet married we have been too intimate.'

"His raised hand prevented her reply.

" 'Let me finish,' he rushed on. 'We have stayed out late of an evening and have otherwise too often been alone together. As yet we have done no wrong. But exposing oneself to the temptation of yielding to an evil inclination is itself sinful.

" 'Between a man and his wife much is permitted. Between a man and other women, even his future bride, far less. It is as if the partition in the synagogue is meant to be universal. As each of us is a holy vessel, let us separate ourselves from profanity, from the profanation of temptation itself, lest we be defiled.

" 'The authorities agree. Let there be a wall between a man and woman taller than both. If this is impossible, taller than one. If this is impossible, as high as the forehead. If this is impossible, the shoulders. If this is impossible, the waist. If this is impossible, the knees. At least, the barrier, physical or not, must be such as to prevent its being crossed immodestly.

" 'Accordingly, I should not sit beside you on the divan but in a chair opposite. So too at the table, where the object itself as well as distance offers protection. On our outings, a third person should walk between us. If not, we ought to keep to opposite sides of a fence or hedge. If all else fails, a space between, equivalent at least to a stride's length, must be maintained.'

"She stared at him, fearful and incredulous.

" 'I would have my wife neither tainted nor suspected of taint.'

"He was declaiming now, and stunned into silence by fear and sorrow, she fled his presence. Later, confiding in her parents, she was reassured.

" 'A bit extreme,' her father said, 'but not unheard of altogether. And, after all, he means to protect your honor as well as his own.'

"' 'Such things were often discussed in my father's house,' her mother added, giving an all but rabbinical stamp of approval. 'But discussed, is not carried out,' she thought to herself.

"Despite some lingering doubt, the young woman complied with the wishes of her betrothed. Though less intimate than it had been, their relationship was at least correct. If she grew wistful at times—when a fence or hedge prevented her reaching toward him—or, if reaching, when he failed to take her hand— still there was peace between them.

"But as summer came on this peace grew more uneasy. The young man became restless, agitated in his speech and movement. If she reached for the back of her thigh, as she did more frequently now with heat and humidity rising, he turned suddenly away, setting his jaw and pressing his palms together. Before long, brushing crumbs from her skirt produced the same response, later, her bending aside to adjust a button or sash, and finally, any unexpected movement to the right and down. Her petting a goat or plucking a rose disturbed him equally. Proffering the flower, she was met with a defensive wave of his protesting hands and the horror in his eyes. At such times, her heart seemed to drain of blood and collapse upon itself.

"Late in August he spoke again.

" 'I know that the restraints upon us have been difficult for you. I also know that our ultimate happiness will be greater for the challenge. But think, then, how much more complete our happiness would be if the challenge were greater still.'

"Absorbed in this thought, he did not see her head bow beneath the weight of his words.

" 'As we are betrothed,' he continued, 'and as you will come to me beneath the marriage canopy clothed in your innocence, so might you in justice and virtue now conceal yourself beneath a veil.'

"He did not wait for her response, but pressed on.

" 'It is in the spirit of the wall prescribed by our teachers yet softer than the mandated stone. But despite the softness, the delicacy, it is stronger than stone in protecting us both from others and ourselves.'

"He reached into his pocket and removed a folded white cloth. Spreading it upon the back of the chair nearest hers, he watched as she reached a tremulous but compliant hand, drew the garment toward her, and slowly settled it upon her head.

"It fell in soft folds below her shoulders. The fabric was translucent but damasked so that her features appeared as faintly outlined ridges or depressions. One could not tell an eye from an embroidered motif and the mouth and nose were discovered only approximately by the soft, slow pulsations of the cloth. A trembling lip, or furrowed brow, or tear went altogether unperceived.

"The young woman's parents were concerned.

" 'I have never heard of a veil before the wedding day,' her mother protested. 'At most a wig or head covering afterward.'

" 'It is not our custom,' her father said, somewhat ill at ease, 'but among Jews elsewhere, I have heard, one is sometimes worn. We must consult the rabbi.'

"After citing authorities and discussing the relationship between custom and law, the rabbi concluded that such concealment, neither required nor forbidden, was permissible since its intent was sanctification.

"Her parents accepted the verdict. Their daughter acquiesced.

" 'It won't be long until the wedding,' her father observed, comforting her, 'and if he is a little zealous, a little jealous, it is still a fine match.'

" 'For what zealous? Of what jealous?' her mother thought to herself. But aloud she merely sighed as she fastened the veil to her daughter's hair with a pearl-tipped pin.

"The town spoke of little else—more in wonder than condemnation, although the few radicals contended that matters had passed beyond piety to superstition. But the young scholar himself seemed pleased, and despite an occasional tense moment caused by a sudden recurrence of the dreaded movement, he looked forward eagerly to autumn, the New Year, and the wedding that would shortly follow.

"On the Sabbath of Repentance, the first after the New Year, the bridegroom-to-be and his parents were guests at the home of his fiancé. The Sabbath candles shone brightly, aromas of Sabbath foods filled the air, and gleaming in white, the young woman might have been not only a prospective bride but the

Sabbath Queen herself. All seemed touched by a spirit born less of merriment than awe—as befitted the solemnity of the Sabbath preceding Yom Kippur.

"Yet when the soup was served, and the white figure bent slowly to the right, the cloth of her dress rippling sinuously, the young man shuddered. No matter that, as they sat diagonally opposite, the length and breadth of the table stood between them and that all flesh was concealed. But in the midst of pleasant chatter his trembling went unobserved.

"During the meat course, the figure in white again seemed to writhe insidiously before his eyes. Sweat broke cold on his face, the hair on the back of his neck rose stiffly—all unnoticed in the passing clatter of plates and the conversation of Sabbath diners at ease.

"After tea and cakes, amid the psalm preceding the blessings after meals, even as the others reached the height of their hymning, the white form seemed to gyrate convulsively before him once more. At this, face flushed, he crashed a fist upon the board and rose shouting, 'Unclean! Unclean! Unclean! She who is blemished shall not enter the sanctuary! She who is blemished shall not stand before the altar of the Lord! She who is blemished shall not be led beneath the canopy!'

"Convulsing, he fell to the floor among the screaming company, and when his spasms subsided, was carried home. On the morning after the Day of Atonement, the engagement contract was cancelled."

Alter paused. Uncertain that the tale was ended, his visitor, attentive and tolerant until this, asked with near disdain, "And? Did no one live happily ever after?"

The rabbi ignored his tone.

"Two years later, the young woman was married to a prosperous rug merchant of a neighboring province. They had children. I do not know whether any of them survived the war.

"The young man did survive—as a pariah among his people at first, then, leaving the town, as a nomad, living among strangers, alone, a Cain unbranded, useful at times to others, but never to himself."

"And the moral, Rabbi?" the young anthropologist asked dutifully.

Alter sighed.

"It is a matter of diamonds. A diamond with a flaw is worth less than a diamond without—and where, by the way, do you find and how many—but worth less is not worthless. Such a diamond is still a woman of worth; her price is still above rubies. To see the fault only, and not the virtue in which it is embedded, is perversion, falsehood, sin—as it once was called. Here it deprives the woman of reputation, the man of an honorable connection, humanity of the progeny they might have produced—not to mention calling into question the skill and intention of the Creator."

The youthful caller, deliberate, twice shook his head from side to side, then measured Alter with a level gaze.

"On the contrary, the story suggests that the search for perfection is endless, that the pursuit of the ideal is the greatest good. Ultimately, it is less a matter of diamonds than of the high purpose of a philosopher uncompromised against the barter and trade of a dealer in carpets."

For a moment, Alter's eyes filled with ancient sorrow and the lines of his face and form drew downward as if to the grave. Then, looking away, he motioned with a deferential hand acknowledging defeat.

The young man rose and put on his coat.

"A professional observation. Absent an oral tradition, the story is more parable than folktale."

Adjusting his matching cap in the open doorway, he uttered a perfunctory farewell.

Silent, the rabbi closed the door after him, expression unchanged.

Seated once more, he watched as his late guest passed before the window, a darker smudge against the darkening stubble and sky. For a moment, the figure paused to take a rectangle of stiff paper from an inner pocket. He studied it briefly, tore it in irregular quarters, and offered it to the wind. Then, thrusting his hands deep into his coat pockets, hunching his shoulders, and bending at the waist, he strode on and passed from view.

Alter opened a drawer of the desk before him. He felt about, as if for a familiar object, and withdrew a faded photograph. Leaning back in his chair, chin sunk on his chest, eyes closed, he caressed the yellowed pieces of transparent tape.

Markers

As he turned from the gravesite and casually surveyed the landscape of low mounds, stelae, and shrubs, he took little notice of a solitary figure some distance away. But gaze returning in its sweep, he was startled to see the form moving briskly toward him. As the figure approached, that the stranger was a man of about his own age—early to mid 60s—became increasingly clear, as did his being somewhat overweight and ill conditioned—in these respects not like himself at all. Nor, he observed as the other drew up beside him, were they compatible in their dress; his own tailored casual—gray cuffed trousers, navy blazer, and cordovan slip-ons—contrasted wildly with the stranger's tan tweed Norfolk jacket and brown pants woven with a splash pattern that draped their cuffless legs over black canvas Keds high-tops.

"The black beret matches the shoes, at any rate," he conceded silently, as he removed from his own head the black skullcap borrowed for the occasion from the cemetery office and folded it carefully into his breast pocket, "though the multi-striped scarf, colorful as it might be and worn Snoopy style about the neck, matches nothing."

"You are . . . ah, visiting?" the other began, nodding toward the plot behind them. "The one with the tall, dark stone?"

"Yes. My grandfather's," he answered, though wary of his inquisitor.

A smile spread over the other's face and his eyes grew bright.

"Ben Edelson," he announced, thrusting his hand forward more as command than offering.

He placed his hand in Edelson's—not a dead fish exactly, but one still fluttering its gills and flopping about occasionally at the bottom of the creel.

"Theo," he said, "Theo Levin."

Edelson's smile burst into grin as he now clasped Levin's hand in both of his.

"Tell me, he asked, barely able to contain himself, "are you Hannah's Teddy or Esther's Teddy?"

The fish came suddenly to life and leaped from its fleshy container.

"Who is this man," Levin thought, backing off a step or two, "and how does he know the names of my mother and aunt and what my cousin Ted and I were called as children?"

"A mystery we will soon solve," Edelson said, as if reading the unexpressed thought. "Come."

He stepped to Levin, took him by the arm and led him back to his grandfather's grave.

"Isaac Schifrin, yes?"

Levin nodded.

"But can you read the Hebrew?"

"Some," Levin mumbled, shuffling his feet.

"Well, look then—'Yitskhok b'rab Shimon Zvuln'. Isaac son of Simeon Zebulon," Edelson translated. "Though if SZ had come to America, I'm sure he would have been called 'Sam' no matter what. Now, lomir shpatsiren," adding at Levin's vacant stare, "mameloshn for 'let's stroll.'"

He guided Levin by the arm, moving in the direction from which he had come, and paused before a plot about a hundred yards away.

"What do you see?" Edelson demanded.

"More Schifrins," Levin blurted, his voice suddenly high pitched.

"Yes, five or six Schifrins, a couple of yours trulys, a pair of Charneys, a Kossoff, who knows how she got in here—a Charney sister, actually. But here, look."

He led Levin to a marker at the front edge of the plot.

"Let us read."

Levin stooped beside him as they examined the stone.

"'Yisroel b'rab Shimon Zvuln'," Edelson intoned. "Israel son of Simeon Zebulon. My grandfather."

Levin saw one of the points at once.

"Brothers?"

"Brothers."

"Are you certain?"

"Look, Theo, Schifrin might not be so unusual a name hereabouts. But trust me, there ain't too many Shimon Zvulns. Besides, my family here," he gestured toward the graves, "has told me plenty about your grandfather, their Uncle Itsik."

Levin blanched.

"Itsik! My grandmother always used that name. It must be. Brothers!"

The other point rose to realization.

"Then, you and I . . ."

"Right," Edelson interjected, "stick around a while and we'll revive the cousin's club as generation II."

Suddenly animated, Levin hugged his newfound relation hard, if briefly.

"Well, at least we're not kissin' cousins," Edelson observed upon release. "But, here, let me introduce you to the family. "Zeyde, Bobe, Mom and Dad, Aunt Lillie, Uncle Moe—everybody, this is Uncle Itsik's an eynikl . . . grandson ... Teddy—Theo, what's your Hebrew name?"

Levin searched through chips of memory.

"Todres?"

"Todres . . .But which Teddy are you, Hannah's or Esther's?

"Hannah's."

"Okay, we begin again. Everyone, this is Feter Itsik's an eynikl, Todres Khanez."

"What exactly is the point . . . Ben?"

"I'm a formal kind of guy."

A faint smile began to curl at the corners of Levin's lips as he looked his cousin up and down.

"Who likes to dress comfortable," Edelson added. "And you," he went on, "are what, in Ralph Lauren?" He rubbed the fabric of Levin's lapel between his thumb and forefinger.

"Armani actually," Levin replied brushing away the intrusive digits and refreshing the nap of the dark wool.

"Me, I'm eclectic," Edelson said. "The shoes from Runner's Retro; the pants from Time and Time Again Thrift; the coat Salvation Army. Not that I have to. It's a kind of hobby, a challenge mostly. You can pick up great stuff!"

Levin frowned, unconvinced.

"But such foolishness," Edelson went on. "We find each other after a lifetime and the only thing we can talk about is shmates? Come, we'll walk on, turn up a place to sit, and have a face to face, maybe a heart to heart, if we're lucky a soul to soul—unless, of course, you don't do soul to soul on the first date."

Levin smiled and permitted himself to be led along the narrow pathways.

"Lots of benches scattered about," Edelson observed. "Granite mostly—like the monuments. But a block to the right the Davidovs have one of wrought iron—I don't know how this was permitted—and over on Mt. Carmel, between Jeremiah and Joshua, there used to be a wooden one opposite the Krinskys. Which is crazy, because in no time at all—thirty or forty years—it rots out. Careful—the Scheinfeld steps jut out nearly a foot into the road. Let's turn left here at Mt. Moriah."

As they walked and he listened, Levin gawked here and there both in response to Edelson's spiel and of his own volition—as if he were, in this setting, a resident of the Great Plains on a first visit to Manhattan. He rubbed his neck briefly as Edelson continued the tour.

"Now, there's one at the Merman-Zelkow place. But look, white spots. Benches under trees are not a good idea. Come along. At the end of the block another left onto Ezekiel—if the procession ahead isn't turning off there—no, see they're headed toward Mt. Nebo—we'll find one nice and clean out in the open."

They walked through the scattering cloud of dust raised by the cortege just passed and made their turn.

"About a third of the way on the right. See?"

As they approached, Levin could read the family name carved at the edges of the seat. Edelson took no notice of this, but planted himself on the bench and with a firm grasp of his cousin's wrist urged Levin down beside him. "Thank you, Mr. Yesner, Mrs. Yesner," he said without a trace of irony, turning toward the graves and touching his beret with his free hand as he spoke.

Released and adjusting a shirt cuff, Levin observed, "You seem to know the neighborhood—and the neighbors"—he nodded toward the Yesners—"very well."

"Neighborhood? Neighborhood!" Edelson's voice hovered between incredulity and indignation. "Theo, take a look around. It's no neighborhood. It's a ward, a district, a borough of the huge city that takes up half of Long Island. This is *it*; welcome to Necropolis, baby! And these," he went on, spreading his arms as if to embrace, "aren't neighbors; they're friends, countrymen—the entire extended family, and Necropolitans every one. And as for knowing—what mayor"—he bowed slightly—"wouldn't know his precincts and his people!"

Levin's stare, a blend of disbelief and alarm, punctured the peroration.

"Teddy, Teddy,' Edelson sighed sinking back, "I'm not altogether crazy. City of the dead—mayor—metaphors—farshteyst? Poetry. In part. In part. But never mistake passion for madness."

He paused, letting his last remark sink in, then casual and brightening, began again.

"So, tell me. You come here often?"

Levin burst at once into raucous laughter until, remembering where he was, he tried to stifle it behind a hand. But Edelson had already recognized the unintended absurdity of the cliché and joined in.

"It's all right," he said, pressing gently on Levin's arm to remove the hand from his mouth, "we're all heymish—down home—here. We can take a joke. Besides," he added, looking Levin up and down, "you're not exactly my bowl of borsht."

Levin laughed again, the sound more subdued, and without reaching for his face.

"Actually," Edelson remarked, "I'm pretty sure of the answer. If you were a regular, I would have noticed you long ago."

"Only twice before," Levin said. "Once, as a child and again much later, more than twenty years ago."

"So what brought you then and what brings you now?"

"Then, my family—Mom, Aunt Esther, the other sisters, cousins (the other 'Teddy' too). They wanted us to see where our grandfather was buried. This was just before they all left the city for Westchester and the Jersey suburbs. The youngest of us had not been to the funeral—I must have been three or four when he died.

"The second time, Mom wanted to come. Dad was gone by then—almost half their generation really—so I drove her."

"You didn't know him, then, Uncle Itsik—your grandfather?"

"Not really. I have a vague memory of a man with a fedora and a cigarette leaning over my crib and another of his giving me something—a little silver cup—I've been told—when he was on what must have been his deathbed."

"You've been told? So, the cup . . .?"

"Lost in the move probably."

"Pity. Not the cup. That you never really knew him. There I have the advantage. I was very close to mine. Still am," Edelson waved in the general direction of the Schifrin family plot. "But not just him," he went on. "I knew—know—his grandfather and his grandfather's grandfather too—just not so close."

"You have a fine head for remembering people you couldn't possibly have met."

"Well, there's memory and there's memory! What can I say? Look, if you're part of the mishpokhe, you 'know' the whole family. As our black friends might put it, these are all the brothers and the sisters."

Levin smiled skeptically. "I'm afraid my acquaintance is more limited."

"I can see. You should get out more. But still, here you are. Because . . .?"

"A farewell visit, you might say. I'm leaving New Jersey and probably won't be back—not very often anyway."

"So, for auld lang syne, eh? Well, maybe we should drink to that."

Edelson drew a small flask from the patch pocket of his coat. Levin stared briefly until a light bulb of recognition went on behind his eyes.

"Wrong," Edelson observed as he unscrewed the cap. "Drinking explains nothing. I carry this as part of the ensemble and because of occasional chill on autumn days like this. And trust me, the family doesn't mind. If, when he leaned over your crib with that cigarette, you had checked out Uncle Itsik's other hand, you might have found a schnapps. So, L'khaim!"

He drank, a mouthful somewhere between a sip and a swig, "aahed," then handed the flask to his cousin.

Levin wiped the rim with a neatly folded pocket square uttered the requisite "L'khaim" then drank himself. This time there was no "aah."

"What is this swill? Manischewitz?"

"Schapiro. Extra special reserve. Last bottle of the last case."

Levin stared at him as if he had been suckered into drinking lye.

"Look, I'm sorry if it isn't to your taste. But when in Necropolis . . ." he began, then trailed off and changed course. "Listen, I know what's what with the vintages. I read the *Spectator* and a couple of times a year ship a case in from California. Still, I'm peasant enough to prefer generic Côtes du Rhône to an estate bottled Bordeaux—Saint-Émilion, say, most of the time. So give me a little credit. Besides, he grinned, "instead of the grape syrup it could have been shlivovits."

"Oh yes, the plum brandy," Levin recollected, having recovered from the unpleasant surprise and duly impressed by Edelson's modest oenophilia. "No doubt it would have been fine Napoleon shlivovits at that."

"The finest. Czech white lightnin'. Nothing's too good for the family."

They settled into comfortable silence, each tilting his head to catch the afternoon rays of a diminished sun. Once or twice Levin turned to gaze at a distant procession or, nearer, at an odd visitor or two. Still sunning himself with eyes closed, Edelson resumed.

"Retired?"

"More than a year."

"From?"

"Real estate."

"Real estate?" Edelson opened his eyes and drew himself up.

"Yes, commercial. Low rise office space, strip malls."

"Me too." He reached an arm toward the scene before them. "But strictly residential."

Levin snorted.

"So what did you do, really?"

"Do, not did. I'm still at my day job. Neuropsychiatrist, would you believe?"

He looked at a still skeptical Levin.

"I wouldn't either. Teacher. High school. Earth Science. Master's plus 30, but the 30 is in linguistics—semantics concentration. The board didn't care; they go by numbers."

"Kids?"

"Too often a pain in the nether regions, but . . . oh, you mean my kids! Three, boy girl boy. One in the Heights, one in Manhattan, one on the Island. Doctor, editor, sociologist. Two married. Four grandchildren. You?"

"Two daughters. One in Vancouver, the other in Zurich, for now. Import/export and international banking."

"The banker. She knows about the Holocaust accounts?"

"It's an American firm. Wouldn't be her department anyway. Wife?"

"Wife? You remember those autograph albums we used to get at graduation. In hers and mine every other page read 'Roz and Ben 4-ever'. A prediction even better than fortune cookies. Not yet forever, but it's getting there."

"My first was not forever," Levin volunteered. "With Jan, it's been only five or six years, so who can tell? And then there's a bit of an age gap."

"Gap?" Edelson asked, holding a thumb and forefinger apart "Or gap?" He spread his arms to full span.

"Gap," Levin said, raising his hand a foot or so above the plane of the bench.

"So, I assume you have insurance?"

"Life?"

"Pre-nup."

Levin nodded.

"Zurich," Edelson considered after a pause. "Well, a six or seven hour flight. . ."

"Longer once I move."

"That's right, you are leaving Jersey. For?"

"Florida. Boynton Beach."

"Florida? Florida! Don't tell me, an over 55 condo community."

"Why not? Great weather, golfing, fishing . . .

"I hear the dying ain't bad either."

Now Levin gestured toward the scene.

Edelson shook his head. "Ratios."

"I'm going there to *live,*" Levin asserted with some heat.

"You'll still pay for perpetual care."

"But until then I have sunshine and exercise in the great outdoors."

"Look," Edelson took up the challenge, "it's not like we have no outdoors up here. Beaches from Coney Island to the Hamptons and parks all over the place—Central, Prospect, Van Cortlandt, Valley Stream, Heckscher—I could go on. And where we are right now is not exactly four walls with central air."

"Right now, we are sitting."

"All right," Edelson rejoined, rising abruptly. "Let's walk some of these nature trails."

"Nature trails?" Levin kept his seat.

"The flora and fauna of Necropolis. Grass and assorted evergreens we have plenty. We are especially big on yew. Sycamores and oaks along the fences. Here and there a maple. Large animals we lack—no 'gators. But squirrels, chipmunks (though they are shy), and rabbits, which you can see frequently at dusk, are present in some numbers."

By now, Edelson was a teacher in performance.

"Insects abound. Ants, beetles, cicadas, butterflies, crickets, grasshoppers. Fish, I admit we're short, but how far is it to the Atlantic? Birds are plentiful. Gulls forever crossing between sea and sound—crows, grackles, finches, sparrows, mourning doves—naturally.

"And speaking of birds," he went on, recovering both his seat and more intimate tone, "let me tell you about something I saw not two years ago. It was a winter day in one of the outlying districts. Snow covered the ground. Someone had come to visit an old friend, a birder. In his honor, the visitor had strewn several fistfuls of birdseed around his place. In minutes the congregation arrived. Blue jays, cardinals, a brown thrasher, nuthatches, sparrows—always sparrows, a dozen chickadees with their black yarmulkes, more than a minyen by themselves. Such flitting, such hopping, such pecking . . ."

"All right, Uncle! You have outdoors, but meandering among shrubs and butterflies is hardly exercise, and flitting, hopping, and pecking—you have told me yourself—is for the birds."

Edelson sighed and shook his head.

"Exercise? I'll tell you what I do. You know the Strand bookstore at 12th and Broadway?"

"I've heard of it."

Edelson glanced at his companion, eyes tinged with pity and regret.

"They say that they have eighteen miles of books. On Monday or Tuesday, I start at the ground floor and work my way to the top floor and back, maybe ten or twelve times, and on every floor walk the aisles of filled bookcases. Of course, I stop now and then, to leaf through a volume or two—or three. A couple of days later, I do it again.

"Low impact aerobics."

The lowest. But with the steps and the bending and stretching to reach shelves it's definitely some limbering up. Besides, there is the acquisition of miscellaneous information—I won't call it knowledge—about cost accounting, Peruvian tin mines, General Beauregard, needlepoint, and leprosy—you name it. Though from this one can get a bad case of browser's thumb." He showed Levin his callus.

"So, it's intellectual exercise."

"In a manner of speaking. But more of a warm up for the cultural. Think of it, Theo, everything from the Brooklyn Academy to Broadway—well, off Broadway these days—the museums, the galleries, Lincoln Center, Carnegie Hall . . ."

"Yes, but what music is there in this Necropolis of yours?"

There was a lengthy pause before Edelson replied.

"Just that. Silence too is part of the great symphony."

Responding to Levin's blank stare, he went on.

"Sorry, Theo. I assumed you were a postmodern man. You know, John Cage and all that." He paused, awaiting a reply that never came. "Strand, music and music theory."

Levin's expression did not change.

"Well, look, just something I picked up browsing."

The pair lapsed into silence once more, whatever tension eased by observing at some slight distance the recessional from Mt. Nebo, cars and a few feet again raising dust along the trail. When they had passed, Edelson renewed the conversation.

"We were talking culture. There's our own too, of course. The Jewish Museum, the Holocaust Memorial, the Tenement Museum, a chunk of Ellis Island, he rattled off. You know, there's still a Yiddish theater, and YIVO—the Yiddish institute—is going strong, to say nothing of schools, shuls, centers, organizations, and the 92nd Street Y. Artists, actors, writers, musicians—just like here."

"Like here?"

"Sure like here. Everybody from Rabinowitz and Cahan to Yesner are in residence."

"Yesner, I know . . . I have met . . . I am aware of," Levin groped. "But you haven't 'introduced' me to the other two."

"Rabinowitz, aka Sholem Aleichem. The *Fiddler on the Roof* stories," he added at Levin's expressionless gaze. Cahan, a novelist, but mostly founder of the *Forward*."

"The old socialist rag?"

"Still around—online now—Yiddish and English—but not exactly socialist these days. And never a rag. No, Abe C. would not be happy with your stockbroker or with my financial adviser. Yes, I have one, would you believe! But it's all in the point of view. To me, the stocks and bonds are just the 21st century version of money in a mattress or a shoebox. OK, so I'm in denial on this," he confessed at Levin's smirk.

"But two things I can affirm," Edelson forged on. "First, we did not come here for the beluga in Bystrom Beach or for the quiche in Clearwater—or, for that matter, to wear white shoes anywhere to dinner at five. And second, this is where it's at."

"This? This *is* only a place for what *was*. I'm looking ahead."

"Ahead? Theo, there is no ahead. There are just two kinds of future. The future that is now and the future to which the past is prologue. Also now. There is no now without a then. And this, this is the then that is my now."

He waited for Levin to absorb what he could and then continued.

"But for you, there, there is no then, and then-less what future could you possibly have?

"Ben, I don't have to live in Necropolis . . . live in a particular place, I mean, to be in touch with the past. Believe me, I carry it with me," he touched his forehead and chest, "here and here."

"Theo, not to impugn your personal memories, which I grant without question, but how much else is there? The *Forward* you knew, but not Cahan; Rabinowitz you knew from *Fiddler*, indirectly. And these are two of the biggies. You told me yourself that you haven't been here for twenty years. Maybe you thought about it in Paramus, Teaneck . . ."

"Used to be Paramus. Short Hills."

"Short Hills?" He studied Levin briefly, noting the manicure and sculpted cut of hair that resisted the movement of a passing breeze. "So, in Short Hills you thought about it. I often think about lemon meringue pie—the appearance, the texture, the taste, but until the fork penetrates that delicate topping, dense filling, and flaking crust and the morsel is in my mouth, I ain't got no sweetness."

"I'm glad you don't teach English."

"Theo, when in Necropolis, I appear in linguistic dishabille. The point is it has to be experienced—ongoing. You can't lock it up in some closet" (he tapped his own head and chest) "and bring it out for inspection—even introspection—twice a year, a decade, a century. It's like that radio station—all news all the time.

"Or maybe it's like the web. You have your own personal computer with memory to the max, but unless you're online, connected, you have only what's in your own little box. And to me, that's what you will have in Boylston Beach, boxes—side by side maybe, maybe on the same shelf, but they don't talk to each other except, again maybe, what it was like—then.

"*Then*, you hear! The past is not that to which the present is prologue. How's that for English? Backwards! Altogether impossible! And you were talking about the future!"

"First," Levin began, both irked and amused, "it's Boynton Beach. Second, where are you preaching tomorrow? Third, if you've never been to Florida, which I assume is the case, how are you such an expert on what's there?"

"Educated guess—mostly. But I know what you don't have." He jerked a thumb toward the adjoining graves. "You don't have Yesner."

"I'm sure there are Yesners in . . ."

"No, no, let me explain," Edelson broke in. "Tell me, you've met your neighbors in the condo?"

"Some."

"What's their background? What did they do?"

"Of the ones I've met, we have a mortgage broker, a principal, a jeweler, an insurance salesman . . . I can't remember what else/"

"These are the men, I suppose. And their wives?"

"The principal's wife was a teacher. The mortgage broker's wife was in real estate."

"Convenient."

"The salesman's was a housewife. The jeweler's, part time in the business, the rest at home."

"Housewives. A vanishing breed," Edelson mused. "But it is

the single largest occupation among Necropolitans. The rest we have too. Jewelers, principals—teachers by the thousands, and the others. But now you make an educated guess. You tell me whether you think you have any of these in your development. We'll play go fish. You remember?"

Levin smiled indulgently.

"So, any corner grocers?"

"Go fish."

"Any candy store keepers?"

"Fish"

"Any tailors, cobblers, peddlers?"

"Fish thrice."

"Thrice? Butchers, bakers, cigar makers?"

"Go."

"Union organizers, seamstresses, sample card makers, ice men?"

Beckoning, Levin urged him on.

"Scholars, felons (white collar doesn't count), floor layers, beadles, corsetieres, failed farmers, blacksmiths, countermen, moving men, laundrymen, washerwomen?"

"How do you expect us to have all these?" Levin protested. Most of the jobs no longer exist or haven't been done by . . . 'the family' for ages."

"Exactly! We all know that cream rises—and clogs those arteries for which there is no Lipitor. Or, try it another way," he began again. "You and your condo friends are living, so to speak, on the upper floors. Not the penthouse—reserved for the corporate lawyers and the CEOs—but below you? Where's the basement? The foundation? There's no living on slabs—really. But Necropolis has it all—all those I mentioned, plus the ones you mentioned, plus some we haven't mentioned—moyels, for example—wrong demographic, yes? And, of course, Yesner and his missus," Edelson concluded, bowing in the direction of their double headstone.

"All right, I'm game. What did the Yesners do that we're missing out on?"

"Ran a pickle stand."

"A pickle stand!"

"A pickle stand and never with the look of sour disdain I now read, Theo, on your face."

"Ben, I respect the hard work and enjoy a good pickle as much as the next . . ."

"It's not the pickle qua pickle," Edelson interrupted. "Not the pickle in *esse* (or in esik—that's vinegar, Theo). Whether cucumber, cabbage, or pepper, whether sour, half sour, sweet or hot—it was not the thing in itself, but its pickleness.

"Picture our grandfathers at dinner—a piece of boiled beef (in good times), a mound of potted potatoes, a chunk of bread, some tap water, seltzer, or tea to wash it down. The almost unvarying menu—chicken soup and chicken on the Sabbath, okay. Monotony. Boredom. But add a pickle, a couple of forkfuls of kraut, half a pepper from the Yesners or the deli and instead of mere edibles you have a meal. Instead of eating, dining.

"And this beyond the dinner table. In the humdrum of their daily lives, routines, some moment of joy—a wedding, a birth, a graduation added its zest, briefly but deeply, and helped them go on. Uncle Itsik, I know was not at your Bar Mitzvah. Maybe your grandmother, Tante Bashe, was? Or grandparents from your father's side?"

Levin nodded.

"So for them, as for my grandparents, this was such a moment. Pure joy, pleasure, delight—a word we don't use much anymore. Something that not only made everyday life bearable but justified it, vindicated.

"By the way, I still have my Bar Mitzvah album. There's a picture of your parents at a table with your aunts and uncles. They look very happy and not just mugging for the camera. Would you care to guess what's on the table besides the cutlery and flowers?"

"Pickles?"

"An enormous bowl."

"So, the pickle as poetry."

"What poetry? They're real pickles!"

"No metaphor?"

"No, real juicy pickles! But . . ."

"But what?"

"Zen," Edelson grinned.

Deflated, Levin shrank momentarily into himself until drawn to attention by the drone of a plane circling low in its descent toward one of the airports. Together with Edelson, he followed the craft until it disappeared in a bank of gray clouds.

"We've never met till now," Levin observed after the pause, "but this afternoon might be enough for a lifetime."

"Precisely," Edelson agreed, but sidestepped his antagonist's thrust. "First, I always give full measure—not less than 37 or 38 inches to the yard. Second, with you headed south, this stands an excellent chance of being our only chance. Maybe 40 inches, then. Besides, though the family might adhere to ritual, customs, or folkways, we do not among ourselves stand collectively on ceremony. So, for my part, it's hail khaver—friend—cousin, in your case—well met."

"How is it," Levin wondered after a moment, "that we never knew each other all these years?"

"Centripetal force," Edelson replied without pause. "Forces, rather. The opposing pulls of increased physical distance (who wants to shlep an hour and a half up the Hudson or across?), of loyalty to the other sides of our families, of bonds to subsets within either side, of friends, schoolmates, interest groups, material disparities and, to some extent, the politics associated with them. Most of all, the American elevation of the individual over the communal. What this country and We need is a good shtetelular centrifuge—as a counter, a balance."

"So, you had your answer before I asked my question."

Edelson gave the scout salute. "Troop 436."

"But how is it," Levin went on, ignoring his cousin's remark and pose, "that you knew about me while I, at best, was only dimly aware of you? I mean, I knew Mom had cousins and that they probably had kids, but they—you were an abstraction."

"It always seemed my business to know. You don't just fall into being mayor. You grow into it—a rite of maturation and initiation at once.

"Maybe it comes of living in a three-room flat, overhearing the chatter of adults when they think you're asleep. Or when clearly awake and present, deciphering their pig Latin, or knowing more of their second language than you let on. Maybe it's gathering in some kitchen on Friday night with a dozen others and by the electric campfire of a 40-watt bulb absorbing the lore, domestic, local, international; and later in the dark of your own dreams making connections among the bits and pieces new and stored.

"This was how I first came to know our friends here and to see all who were not yet here—you included—as potential residents. Which all of us, in the end, are. The law of return—again—from a different exile."

"So is that all there is, Necropolis and its way station, New York? A while ago you said I should get out more."

"As Thoreau says in *Walden*," he checked Levin's face for a glimmer of recognition but settled for its impassivity, "'I have traveled much in Concord'—the town in Massachusetts, not the grape." He patted the flask through thick tweed.

"Still, I get around. The mayor might not get a vacation, but the teacher does, two months in summer, two weeks at least during the school year. Yes, there is a world—of sorts—beyond the Hudson. And I've been there. Those cases of California wine? I don't order them by throwing darts at pictures in a catalog. I've been to Napa and Sonoma—done the tastings and tours. I've been to Yellowstone and the Grand Canyon. I've seen the home where the buffalo roam—or used to. San Francisco, Santa Fe, Chicago; Canajoharie, Williamstown, Ogdensburg—for their museums, to say nothing of those in Florence, Rome, Paris, London and Amsterdam. I've had breakfast in Perrysburg, Ohio, lunch in Pompeii—it was rather good, dinner in Sydney harbor. Shall I go on?"

Levin signaled him to stop.

"Fine," Edelson continued, "no more tripping. But wherever I go, I am who I am. New Yorker, yes, but Necropolitan through and through. And I don't mean counting the Cohens and Levines in the white pages. This is a diversion. Damned short one too in Canajoharie and Ogdensburg.

"Put simply, maybe crudely, it's the perspective of thousands of years, down countless generations ongoing, an essential distillation of all their diversity of times, places, languages. So I have been out there, done this and that. But it's never just me meeting the world on its terms; it's also the world meeting me on mine."

He wheezed and paused to catch his breath.

"Ben, your nature walks and book patrols may be pleasant, but you really need to work out."

"So too says my wife, my doctor, and my son the doctor. Can you believe such a cliché? Well, you're all probably right. So, since you're leaving the area, and he'll have a hole in his schedule, let me have the number of your personal trainer. Maybe I'll put in a call, and he can recommend someone in my neck of the woods."

"How do you know I have a personal trainer?"

"Your having and my knowing both come with our respective territories."

After consulting his phone's contact list, Levin produced a notepad and fountain pen, wrote a name and number, and handed over the slip of paper.

"Parker?" Edelson asked as Levin replaced the pen cap.

"Caran d'Ache. Swiss, a gift from my daughter."

"I'd lose it in half a day," Edelson observed. He drew a stick pen from the pocket that held the flask. "BIC. Does the job and keeps the dollar store in business. This is not perverse pride. Just can't hang onto things. What I should do," he said as he returned the pen to his pocket, "is carry a bottle of Waterman's and a quill. But that would be pretentious, an affectation."

He looked at the paper Levin had given him. "Jeri with an 'i.' How personal does the training get."

"Personal, not intimate. Jeri with an 'i' is married to Bruno with a 'B.'"

"Curiosity is not necessarily interest. Thanks." Edelson stuffed the slip into his wallet among a half dozen crumpled bills. "But what can I give you?"

"You have already given me an earful," Levin replied. "Let's call it an exchange of gifts."

"Generous of you, Theo. Not to be crass or ungrateful, but generosity aside, I'm not sure how valuable a promise or possibility I've evoked might be—left unfulfilled. Yet, if rejected or discarded, it can't, at least, be sold. I've never seen an ad for such a thing—not even during a store closing or January sales."

Through the uneasy moments that followed, the pair distracted themselves by watching the late afternoon sun in its slow descent toward the horizon and the movement of a stray cemetery pickup truck or van as it negotiated the narrow pathways of the grid. After a time, Edelson began tapping contemplative fingers against the bench. Finally, resolved, he turned to Levin and said, "I have a confession to make."

"Oh?"

"I've been to Florida."

"Well, you can't be forgiven unless you forgive yourself," Levin jibed.

"This is really not a question," Edelson replied. "But," he went on with exuberance rising, "It was not the Florida that you know—the Barton beaches or whatever. And it wasn't Miami or Orlando either.

"Years ago, I was in the Everglades for two weeks. The board somehow got a grant to send a few of its science teachers for what they called 'enrichment.' I was 'enriched,' but not in any way they intended. They wanted us to gain hands on, or at least first-hand experience with the wildlife, the plants, the ecosystem down to water level and flow and to soil variety and density. But what I got was a sense of the primordial and, paradoxically, how it is at once essential and antithetical to civilization and culture.

"Yes, I made notes on the alligators, coral snakes, chiggers, mangroves, took pictures of these and of the evidence of a panther that none of us actually saw. Mere details. What impressed were the drive to live and the necessity of death in order to achieve that life.

"This understanding is my chief qualification for public office. Not that we have rejected the primitive. Such a thing is impossible. But we have built upon it, layer upon layer, interconnection upon interconnection so that we have made it obscure and inaccessible. The pelican snaps up a fish and swallows it whole. We have it caught, processed, prepared, and served by four different people and unless it's served with head and tail, see the meal as some abstraction, as "fish" not as a particular pompano or trout, say—a once living creature. And even Miller's Analogies can't come up with one for what tuna salad is to tuna."

"There's a lot of quicksand in the Everglades. Nothing you want to build on."

"Emes—true. Life is dangerous, risky, treacherous. Not so death. The Yesners here," he reached to touch their stone, "remain without fear that some pelican hand of a passing ten-year-old will swoop into one of their barrels and make off with a half sour."

"The Yesners, I'm afraid, are out of the loop."

"Not so. They are the closing of the loop. Full circle. According to the ancient Greeks, a perfect form. Anyway, I wanted to be completely up front about Florida."

"Candor appreciated, but as you say, it's not the Florida I know."

As he spoke, Levin consulted his watch. "Well, looks like I'll be caught in rush hour."

"Not here you won't. Sometimes the streets are a tight squeeze, but no one's in a hurry and there's no blocking the box."

"I remind you, I'm heading away from Necr . . . here."

"Temporarily. By the way, nice watch. Movado, no?"

Levin nodded.

"Now, if you can get rid of that dot and the two hands, you'll really have something."

"If I got rid of the dot and the two hands, all I'd have is a watch face."

"You'd have timelessness, infinity, perfection."

"Then why would I bother wearing it?"

"Precisely!" Edelson said. He pushed each of his sleeves up in turn to expose his bare wrists.

"And if you want to know the time?"

"I rarely do. At home, I admit, mornings I sometimes use the clock radio alarm. But at school, they set off bells. And here they close at sunset, which is whenever, depending on the season. If I overstay, they throw me out."

"Someone throws out the mayor?"

"It's more like a strong recommendation. You know, like the secret service recommending that the president stay in the car or go on foot or whether to take this route or that." As he spoke, he spotted a figure waving to him at some distance and waved back.

"That was one of the groundskeepers giving the signal now. Which still leaves us ten or fifteen minutes. Come, we'll make haste slowly and look in on a few folk as we head back."

As they rose, Edelson offered a parting salute to the Yesners and motioned Levin to continue in the direction in which they had originally been headed.

"We move like chess pieces. Knights. One square up to Mt. Zion, then two over to Zechariah. What? You never played?" he asked, at Levin's puzzled expression.

"Not in fifty years."

"Me, not since the kids were teenagers. But you never forget, like riding a trolley car."

"You mean a bicycle."

"Never had one."

"What's there to riding a trolley car?"

"Theo, I don't mean pay your fare and sit down. I mean jumping on the back and hanging on till you're caught or you reach your stop. Speaking of which, Weiss here," he paused before an oddly tapered stone, "used to run a deli at the end of one of the lines. Had great hands, I'm told. You remember those paper cones they used to put mustard in? I've heard he could wrap a hundred in less than three minutes."

"So, one man's claim to fame," he observed as they went on. "But the children acknowledged it, however humorously. By their distinctions shall ye know them."

"If that's the case, you won't be forgotten either."

"Wouldn't it be interesting," Edelson replied, ignoring the personal comment, "if every marker actually symbolized characteristics and attributes of their owners? We turn here. A blackjack player might have a pair of aces doubled down, an avid reader a stack of books . . . But no," he paused, "council would never approve. And they'd be right. Too much visual clutter."

"Council?" Levin asked, above the crunch of fallen leaves beneath their feet.

"What did you think? That I ran the place alone? A tyrant? I am simply first among equals, a benevolent oligarchy of philosopher kings.

"But the truth is," he picked up the thread, "we all mark our territories, so why not here? Take a look at Sonya Diamant, on the left, her photograph fixed to the monument. A lot of the Russians do that. Brightens things up a bit. Takes the edge off the gray. We too have our shifts in style—our fashions *du jour, d'année, de siècle, d'éternité*."

"Don't forget *liberté* and *égalité*," Levin quipped.

"Never. And *fraternité* goes without saying."

They walked on amid the lengthening shadows. Silent now, their footfalls and the twitter of an odd bird or two the sole sounds. Random movement in the middle distance caught their eye.

"Rabbits," Edelson resumed, "like I said." Then, changing the subject, "Have you noticed the mushrooms?"

"Mushrooms? These were not in your list with the yews and sycamores."

"Not mushroom mushrooms. Look, those little white tablets that protrude not half a foot above the ground. There, to your right, for instance. Sometimes I call them that. It saves on wet sleeves and Kleenex. Stillborns or infants too young to have been named. Our unknowns.

"And sometimes—with the usual stone and inscription— their older brothers and sisters—eight years old, ten, fourteen. If you study the dates maybe you can tell what kind of polio season it was. Or here, as we turn into Zechariah and meet the Moldovskys—see for yourself."

Levin studied the plot of ten.

"All of them? In the same year?"

"In less than three months.

"Why? How?"

"The date, Theo, the date. 1918."

"My God, the flu! The Great Pandemic."

"Sounds like the name of some magician. This one turned a lot of us into Necropolitans. Sometimes, cousin mine, the job is depressing."

Now contemplative, they shuffled as much as walked the next fifty yards or so along the leaf strewn path, until stopping once more and pointing to his left, Edelson said, "Not exactly cheerful either."

Levin read the inscription: Aaron Belfus, Beloved Son, Uncle, Friend, January 18, 1922-March 11, 1943. "Soldier?"

"Most likely. More of these too. But at least there was a purpose. Two, really, for us. But take heart, Theo," he brightened. "We have one more stop."

"Permit me," Edelson began as they paused just short of the next intersection, "to introduce Mendel Koenigsberg, oldest resident in these here parts."

Levin made out the weathered but still legible date. "d. 1874. I'm impressed."

"As you should be," Edelson replied. "Old Mendel beat the Great Wave by six years and must have been here before that. Maybe not so long as most uptowns and no way the New Amsterdamers. But, hey, us Schifrins didn't know from the Dutch West India Company—unless you've got stock?"

"Ben, they've been off the board for some time."

"I'll take your word. No time to follow the market. Managed accounts. Here, take my money and run—but not too far."

Levin squinted ahead of them. "I can just make out the office and parking lot in the last of the light."

"We're into the homestretch now. Your feet holding up in those slippers?"

"Loafers."

"Same difference. A trek through space and time requires sound footing."

"Time, too?"

"It's a continuum. Haven't you heard?"

Levin twitched a tentative smile.

Edelson glanced toward him. "Leaf on your shoulder."

Levin reached to remove it but was prevented by his cousin's thick hand.

"Not just a leaf. *Ulmus americana.* American elm." Edelson looked left and right, futilely. "Well concealed. Large tree, too, at full growth."

"Maybe it's a young Marrano," Levin offered.

"Not bad, coz," Edelson replied, patting Levin on the back vigorously. "Still," he considered, "I award only half credit. Hidden maybe, but an elm is not pretending to be a spruce."

He whisked all traces of the leaf from Levin's jacket.

"So this is a test," Levin replied, feelings ruffled despite his garment's being smoothed.

"Not in the least. Unless," Edelson qualified, "in the sense of comparing to a standard. Like playing a round of golf by yourself—no partner, no opponent—just the course. A hole in one by some magic, four quintuple bogies—by some miracle so few. Who knows the score? Just you.

"And even in a match, you fill out your own card. Sure, make a mistake and the judges catch you it's a penalty, maybe the big one. Life too. But in the end, it's what you actually did that matters. You do play?"

Levin nodded and smiled. "And you don't?" he asked, as much statement as question.

"No. But I make one negative application from the casual version of the game to my work here. No Mulligans—in whatever sense you like."

As Levin puzzled briefly over the last remark, Edelson returned to examining the leaf.

"Harder and harder to come by with the beetles and blight. A survivor, this one. A worthy specimen for the granddaughter's album, if you don't mind."

Levin shrugged. With some tissues pulled from an otherwise empty pocket, Edelson wrapped the prize carefully, returned the wad, then signaled for them to walk on.

"Our chariots await," he announced as they approached the parking lot. "Which of these paltry few are you?"

"The midnight blue Mercedes."

"Ah, Third Reichsmobile! Me, I'm in a Ford Antisemiticar.

"That was a long time ago, Ben."

"Actually, a bit longer in your case. Dolph Hitler died in '45, Hank Ford in '47—who knows, maybe of grief. Still, one of us gave his purchase a second thought. Could be consciousness rather than ripeness that is all."

Levin withdrew a case from its pocket and presented his card. "Shall we...?"

"Don't use them," Edelson replied. "I can always be found in the white pages—or here. Nevertheless, I will oblige." He recovered his stick pen, turned the card over, and scrawled his name and number on the back.

"Besides," he added, as he returned the card to Levin, yours will be useless once you move to . . ." He paused, groping for words. "Don't tell me. It's with a B, definitely a B. Not Brighton Beach. Absolutely not. Nyetnyetnyet. Boonton. Boonton Beach! How's that?"

"Close enough."

"Regardless, Theo, I know where you live."

"Are you so sure?

"Sure enough."

"So?"

"So, in honor of my beret we take leave of each other in the French manner."

He seized Levin about the shoulders, feinted a kiss on each cheek, then strode off.

Speechless, Levin watched as Edelson jumped into his car, started and revved the engine, then exploded up the driveway. Pulling into the road and apparently alert to Levin's astonished stare, he shouted, "Hey, even a Necropolitan has to live!"

Levin saw moving lips reflected in a rearview mirror, Edelson's upturned palms, and the red Mustang convertible disappear. But at the distance and above the din of passing traffic he had heard nothing.

Reprise

*. . . And when the last Red Man shall have perished, and
the memory of my tribe shall have become a myth among
the white man, these shores will swarm with the invisible
dead of my tribe, and when your children's children think
themselves alone in the field, the store, the shop, upon the
highway, or in the silence of the pathless woods, they will
not be alone. At night when the streets of your cities and
villages are silent and you think them deserted, they will
throng with the returning hosts that once filled them . . .*
— attributed to Chief Seattle

Two instances had preceded all the others. Their discovery,
however, came only as investigations into the occurrences—
more accurately, a series of occurrences over the better part
of a year—were drawing to a close. Oddly enough, these earliest
events had taken place on the same day in mid-July little more
than half a mile apart.

According to Youssef Mickens, owner of a barbershop on
Newland Street, customers and hangers on were chatting and
bantering as usual above the sounds of rap throbbing insistently
from the resident boom box when this music suddenly stopped
and was replaced by a succession of ominous piano chords.

"Don't fuck with the box, man," one of the regulars
commanded.

"I ain't fuckin' with it," the accused protested.

"Then it must be like you, fuckin' with itself."

But first beneath and then above the ensuing laughter, Rachmaninoff's Prelude in C Sharp Minor (identified later by the humming of sometime sideman Antoine Ellis) tolled on, and, to the wonder of those gathered, no pressing of presets or turnings of dials could interrupt it. Moments after the men stopped trying, the cut they had been listening to picked up where it should have in light of the elapsed time. The incredulous inhabitants of Mickens' establishment shook their heads in silent wonder. Only after one of them joked about longhair music in a barbershop needing some trim was any of their usual good humor restored.

Of the two events, that involving the radio was perhaps the less startling. It might have been explained (and later was), though not without some difficulty, by such things as cultural conspiracy on the one hand and signal drift or sun spots on the other. But the affair of the dominoes apparently lent itself to no explanation at all, improbable or otherwise, save sleight of hand.

Estéban Guttierez had been playing with his friends at a folding table set up beside the doorway of his apartment building on Sutcliffe Avenue. Each man stroked one or two of the domino pieces he held as they collectively studied the possibilities laid out before them. Then, all at once, there were no more pieces but cards—clusters in each man's hand arranged by suit and value and a deck in the middle of the table. No one spoke, but all eyes exclaimed "¡Qué pasa!" Catching their breath and clearing their throats with a long draft of the beers that stood before them, they examined the cards and seemed more puzzled still.

"Julio," one called at last, "hey, chico—college man—ven' acá."

Reluctantly setting his book aside, Julio rose from the stoop and shuffled toward the table.

"Look," Estéban said as he handed him the deck. "Qué clase de cartas son?"

The student examined them casually. "Pinochle," he said without explanation and returned to the abandoned volume.

One of the four had heard of the game and shared what information he had. But as he was speaking, Julio called from the stoop, "Hey, if you all don't know what it is, how can you play?"

"A thinker," Estéban jested, tapping his forehead. "Tiene razón. They teach him well at the college."

His mates laughed nervously with little heart. And what little they had was excised by Julio's second question. "You never play cards anyway. Where are the bones?"

To this question neither Estéban nor the others had an answer. One of them crossed himself. Another eyed the mischievous Santiago, a notorious practical joker, perched and smiling atop the hood of a battered Buick.

"¡Tu!"

"Not me, man," Santiago replied, fingers of both hands touched to his chest in posture of angelic innocence though he smiled more broadly still.

Unnerved as they all were, his accuser did not persist. Nor did the dominoes return.

News of the two occurrences remained local, and since neither was repeated, in short order drifted out of conversation and consciousness. But a few weeks later as the neighborhood baked in the heat of an August evening came reports of strange sounds in the vicinity of a mosque and several churches—A. M. E., Baptist, Pentecostal indiscriminately. Those who heard it agreed that it was a sort of music without melody, sorrowful, less a wordless chant than an undulating wail of lamentation that rose and fell with the wind that presaged the coming thunderstorm. Some opined that it was the sound of the wind itself blowing through the oversized windows of these religious establishments and that the variation in pitch corresponded to the differing size of the openings. And so it might well have been.

But in the minds of some the lightning strike at the Baptist Church on Briscoe Street left the matter unresolved. For struck by the bolt, the pallid Star of David, a relic of the building's first inhabitants still visible below the roof line, was engulfed in flames that burned fiercely in the dusk—all the more for lack of light in the church and surrounding buildings, in which power had failed—until the fire was extinguished at last by the downpour. Inspection the following day revealed that the sash of a nearby window had been seared as well as two or three floor planks within. Curiously, despite the heavy rain and elapsed time—half a day at least—thin wisps of smoke drifted faintly about the singed and blackened star as if the fire still smoldered.

The events of the storm created a vague ripple of unease. But those in the weeks immediately preceding and following Labor Day created a more general swell of wonder and apprehension, not only throughout the neighborhood but in some of the others adjoining. This time it was not houses of worship but shoe stores that were involved—and more precisely, those stores selling children's shoes—businesses particularly sensitive at this time of year because of anticipated back-to-school sales.

Over the two-to-three-week interval, shopkeepers arriving at their stores regularly found shippers' cartons awaiting them. None had ordered the goods, which was of two sorts: a. foot-long cardboard cylinders with removable caps, variously colored, tapered at one end and marked to resemble a pencil; b. 8" x 4" zippered pouches made of imitation leather, also in many shades. Each container, regardless of type, held two or three actual pencils, a six-inch wooden ruler, a rubber eraser and a penholder without nib. Some of the pouches held a drawing compass or protractor as well.

The shopkeepers would normally have returned the merchandise, but, except for their business names and addresses, the cartons were unmarked. Nor did they bear any sign of who the carriers might have been. At a loss, some of the merchants decided to distribute these items to their young customers with each purchase. But the inexplicable sounds that regularly accompanied the transfer, those of suppressed, stifled, even strangulated laughter soon discouraged the practice.

Some of the tradesmen attempted to engage the authorities in solving their little conundrum but to no purpose. The police could not see that any crime had been committed, the postal inspectors could not determine whether any of the extant boxes had ever been in authority hands, and the Interstate Commerce Commission saw no reason to go beyond logging the report, a concession in itself since it was impossible to know whether the goods had ever crossed state lines. But the *People's Progressive*, a neighborhood weekly, took public notice of the matter in a three-paragraph filler:

"Local Shoe Shops Puzzled"

Shipments of unordered pencil cases have been arriving at local shoe stores. Neither the storekeepers nor government investigators can explain their arrival, and the shipping cartons have no return address. Such merchandise was once used as giveaways with purchases of children's shoes, but until now this quaint practice had been abandoned for more than fifty years.

Some speculate that the cases are old inventory that made its way to computerized distribution lists and were sent as a result of a programming error. Others contend that the cases and their contents are of recent manufacture. Many believe that the shipments are a practical joke.

But with this added distraction during their busy season, the merchants aren't laughing.

With the school year well under way, however, shipments (if that's what they were) ceased and the pencil case flap settled down to be filed in the collective mind among life's anomalies. And for a month or so the community returned to its usual concerns. But early in October routine was broken once again by what quickly became known as the "new construction." Sporadically, in bare spots across the neighborhood—in empty lots, on piles of rubble left from the leveling of buildings years ago—small huts suddenly and inexplicably appeared. Some were little more than a series of posts connected by chicken wire; others, more substantial, seemed built of scrap—discarded plywood, battered doors long unhinged now nailed together. However varied, the huts had in common a rough table and benches, an opening at one end, and a roof that was merely a crosshatched overlay of cornstalks, reeds, and branches. As puzzling as their presence was that no one ever saw them being built. They were just there, presumably growing in the night like Jonah's gourd.

As more huts appeared and word spread, the similarity of the structures to those temporary buildings erected by Jews at this time elsewhere in the city in celebration of the holiday of Succoth was duly noted. One columnist in the *People's Progressive* suggested that "Hasidic communities to the west might have placed them as a provocation." These groups, however, not only denied responsibility but also took pains to suggest that the "new construction" (as usually described, for they claimed no first-hand knowledge) was perhaps less than orthodox in its design.

Whatever the political ramifications might have been, residents reacted to the structures in their midst in perhaps predictable ways. Some, out of superstitious fear, shunned them altogether. Others burnt a few to the ground. In several, street people sheltered themselves against the increasing chill. And, in many more, children picnicked before or after school, sharing their sugared snacks.

And in a week, all that still remained were gone as suddenly and as inexplicably as they had appeared. Both the homeless and the children were disappointed. And once again the local journal trotted out a conspiracy theory, this time prompting the mayor's office for community affairs to begin some preemptive quiet diplomacy. Perhaps one or two in various municipal posts had already raised an eyebrow with the episode of the huts following so closely upon the affair of the pencil cases.

So far as the public was concerned, the huts, now out of sight, were, like the pencil cases, also out of mind. Besides, a belated heat wave coupled with a sanitation workers' strike posed problems both more urgent and more pungent. Not just the neighborhood, but also the city as a whole, suffered under a pervasive and increasing stench. Marking the first seven days of the dual affliction, a tabloid heading screamed "REEK WEEK ONE!" Another, not to be outdone, countered with "THE SMELL FROM HELL!" But as the heat broke and workers returned to their jobs, both trash and odors disappeared. Except that in the neighborhood two or three overlapping aromas seemed to linger, at first, and then—even after a cleansing rain—intensify: pickle brine, sauerkraut, onion faintly tinged with fish.

Investigators from several health and air quality control agencies noted that the odors were concentrated in two spots—near the intersection of Rockwood and Livermore, particularly at the site of the Jamaica Jerk Hut, and along Eastridge Street north of Newland, with the epicenter at Dos Hermanos Dollar Store. But since, except for onions and some fish, the cuisine at the Hut could not be the source of the problem, and since the Dollar Store sold no items that could have produced the odors, the investigators drew no conclusions. So, as usual, the residents put up with the inconvenience and sometime nasal affront until it dissipated of its own accord—after a sudden (and more seasonable) cold snap and the consequent firing up of heating systems.

With the fragrances of pickled fish and fermented cabbage gone and officialdom ostensibly dealing with previous crises, the upcoming Halloween celebration was foremost in the minds of the populace. To be sure, police presence increased as mischief night approached, but most of the residents were more attentive to finding costumes, arranging parties, and trick or treating. During the late afternoon and early evening of October 31st, children, out in costumed force, expected a hefty haul. Their chatter and cries along with the calls of protective adults chorused through the air, fit accompaniment for the balletic winding along the streets in and out of buildings.

None of them in these earthly pursuits (and very few others) took note of the skies. At the horizon in all directions blue-black clouds, vaguely shaped like cartoon ghosts, seemed to link their wispy arms and as the wind rose and shifted, whirl in a great circle dance, turn and counterturn, until darkness fell.

For nearly six weeks after Halloween there seemed to be a lull, a return to normalcy, if one discounted a number of requests for buckwheat groats in the local food stores just before Thanksgiving. Without question, this minor event had been prompted by the scattered distribution of handbills that touted buckwheat stuffing. But, except for a small rash of phone calls among the merchants, almost none of whom stocked the item—"You mean grits, ma'am? —," the matter raised barely a blip on the radar screen of public consciousness.

Similarly, the matter of the mid-December lights, at first drew little attention, particularly since holiday decorations were again being hung and lit all over the district. Shops and lampposts along Preston Avenue had been festooned and brilliantly ablaze for weeks. So it was perhaps not surprising that only an odd observer or two noticed the first of what seemed to be pale flames rising wraithlike above the tallest of the Rockwood housing project towers and over another complex building along Watling Street. That these, whatever they were, consumed nothing, except in short order themselves, quite possibly led to a shrug or a shake of the head rather than alarm.

But by the third or fourth night, reports had been called in to the police and fire departments. Not only had this brief luminescence appeared again atop the buildings mentioned but above others elsewhere as well. Cursory examination found nothing, neither fire, nor ash, nor signs of excessive heat. If anything, fire inspectors seemed puzzled by patches of roof that were colder still than their surroundings, already seasonably chilled by the frigid air. But the phenomenon recurred for several nights more, apparent flames hovering over each of the buildings previously affected and an additional other. This incremental spread and that their light remained visible for little more than twenty minutes aside, there seemed to be scant pattern to the incidents. Ostensible flames might appear anywhere from sunset to near midnight, and, except for the initial sites, in widely scattered places, as far as Glanville Avenue to the north and Van Sandt eastward.

Lack of evidence notwithstanding, explanations abounded. The most popular (all discussion of witchcraft aside) involved phosphorescence of many sorts (as well as the burning of phosphorus itself), St. Elmo's fire, and the Northern Lights. Expert opinion (the news media by now had been involved) rejected each of these in turn. Further clamor might have arisen had the phenomenon persisted, but in little more than a week the putative flames were gone as abruptly as they had appeared. Relieved of this distraction, the citizenry focused fully on the Christmas celebration that lay immediately ahead.

But two days after the holiday, a fresh report of flickering lights above a single low building on Cheswick Street, suggested a recurrence. Inspectors this time, however, found a probable cause, much to the delight of the *People's Progressive*, which ran the story under the headline "Latest 'Mystery' Solved."

> Fire Inspector Desmond Harris announced yesterday that his department had found the remains of a large block of frozen carbon dioxide (dry ice) atop 409 Cheswick St. The local engine company had responded to a call that reported flames rising from the building. Although when the substance melts it produces a vapor that is more like smoke than fire, caught in surrounding light it could easily appear to be flaming.
>
> Inspector Harris has not only solved this particular puzzle but also, apparently, the puzzle of the 'flames' that troubled the neighborhood for a series of nights earlier this month. The inspector declined to speculate about why anyone would need dry ice at this time of year or why anyone would place it on a rooftop.

The *Progressive* itself declined to speculate on why or how blocks of frozen CO_2 might be placed repeatedly at scattered sites over an eight-day interval.

But the new year brought distractions of its own, as reports of strange figures appearing in the neighborhood began to circulate. Although these were not in any way intrinsically threatening, their odd unfamiliarity itself drew wary attention over several weeks from those who saw them. That all were white was duly noted, and some observers appeared to dwell on the precise skin tone, sometimes remarking on what, to their almost uniformly dark eyes, seemed either excessive pallor or a clarity that bordered on transparency.

The old man with the beard and skullcap bearing a sack of laundry on his back was discounted in some quarters because it had been reported by three habitués of the Lavender Lounge in the wee hours of the morning. But other sightings met with at least somewhat greater credence. A man with a pushcart full of produce was said to have been seen at midday. Some on the scene suggested that it was a construction worker with a wheelbarrow, but these deniers were hard pressed to determine what sort of barrow contents might resemble oranges and lettuce.

Still elsewhere, the story of the woman with the dead chicken was met with somewhat less skepticism. She had been walking along Thayer Street, it was said, humming to herself and plucking the bird she held before her. Witnesses claimed to have picked up some of the discarded feathers. Not that there weren't scoffers—

"Them's pigeon feathers"

"Chicken"

"Pigeon"

"Look, man, I know the difference between chicken and pigeon"

—though such debates ended swiftly with either a playful exchange of hard jabs to the biceps or laughter provoked by tickling with the plumage in question.

Reports by children, however, were typically greeted without demur, possibly because of presumed innocence on the part of the reporters. Almost invariably, these involved the sudden, unexplained appearance of pale strangers, all of whom were children themselves, at a school or playground. One of the most memorable (perhaps because most commented upon) was the blond child who was discovered in the midst of a schoolyard game of dodge ball, causing the boy who was "it" to stop in mid toss and bring his noisy peers to silence. Almost more than her pallor, it was her clothes that drew stares and comments—from the thick gray felt skirt with the embroidered black dog to the black and white saddles on her feet. "Funky," one or two observed at subdued distance, but the tone was as much question as exclamation. When astonishment seemed to give way to some hostility and menace, the girl promptly disappeared.

A similar episode took place at Ramshead Park one mild March day when an apparently white teenager was observed at the edge of the basketball court. One by one the shake and bake, trash-talking slam dunkers (would-be and actual) stopped to stare in silence. The boy, thumbs thrust into his thick black belt, was all in denim, two inches of pants leg rolled up. His hair, perfectly in place and oiled as if it had been lubricated one strand at a time, curled onto his forehead.

Recovering from his initial shock, one of the players called, "Hey, dude, you a white boy who can jump? Let's see your stuff."

He fired a hard pass toward the stranger. Without visible haste, the boy withdrew his thumbs from the belt, caught it, slid one foot toward the other as if it were a dance step, then holding the ball chest high and barely lifting his heels from the ground, shot it with two hands toward the basket twenty feet away. It rattled the remnant metal net resoundingly as it fell through. The players burst into laughter, less at the shot's success than at the style.

"Hey, you must be a old man," his challenger resumed. "Only my granddaddy shoot like that."

But by this time the boy had turned and begun walking toward the gate, displaying the duck's tail of his haircut and his name blazoned on the back of his jacket.

"Oh, that's cool, "one of the players remarked, his gaze passing over the painted Gothic letters, red shadowed with gold. Others mumbled their assent.

"Yo, Larry," the leader called out. The rest took up the name as if it were a chant. "Larr-y. Larr-y." But the object of their mixed admiration and derision merged with the passing traffic and was lost from view.

As the players returned to their interrupted game, one of them remarked, "I seen where he gone, but where the hell do he come from?" To this and the ensuing silence a wicked pass delivered in frustration served as sole reply.

Spring took hold in a matter of weeks, bringing its familiar seasonal change but no cessation of unnerving disturbances. Arriving at work early on a Tuesday morning in April, caretakers at the cemeteries in Cedar Hills were appalled to find a great number of headstones toppled or turned (many in the same direction). Worse still, a number of graves seemed to have been opened. At least an attempt had been made to open them, for several had fissures running irregularly down their centers, as if they were cakes made with a surfeit of leavening. Panicked, the men checked the burial site of the cemeteries' best-known inhabitant, the writer Samuel Temkin. Here the excavation seemed nearly complete, the opening wide and smoothly edged. But, almost perversely, the memorial stone stood intact and in place. Nevertheless, surmising vandals had been at work yet again, one of the workers called the local precinct to report the crime.

"Not the kids this time," he said as he put down the phone. "An earthquake, would you believe? Just 4.6 they said—but still!" He shook his head repeatedly in lingering disbelief.

His colleague was skeptical.

"Nah, not strong enough to do all this. Never even felt it. Did you? Still, quake or kids, we'll just have to put the stones back in place and deal with some patches of grass.

The first remained bewildered.

"But old Sammy, now," he puzzled, "grave's wide open, but where's the fill?"

Within the hour, however, a small dump truck bearing a huge mound of fresh soil, seed, and cuttings of new sod, drew up to the writer's grave site; and in an hour more, the great Temkin was returned to the serene dignity that had long been his.

Throughout the morning and well into the afternoon, crews shoveled, raked, tamped, or planted at the plots of lesser lights, undoing the minor ravages whatever the cause. When the final grave had been restored and the last stone righted, a pair of groundskeepers sat in a rear office checking their work orders against a master list. As they dealt with the few remaining names, the wind, which had been at calm, rose softly out of the east, now a melancholy flute, now a mournful cello in its sigh and sough.

"Jonah Lipmann."

"Done."

"Berel Malisoff."

"Done."

"Ida Bessen."

"Done."

"Ezra Lutz."

"Done."

"Bernard Fiedler"

"Done."

"Annette Monder."

"Done."

"Reuben Lutwak."

"Done."

"Rachel Neidig."

"Done."

"Rosalind Solow."

"Done."

"Morris Ittelson."

"Done."

"And done."

At this, the wind gusted momentarily as if in crescendoed affirmation, ruffling the pages fixed to the several clipboards. A workman closed the window, but a breeze persisted in muffled, solemn chant through the budding trees.

These events ascribed to the small tremor were the last of the curious circumstances that had occurred in the neighborhood since the previous July. However, the official investigation launched at the appearance of the huts continued for many weeks longer. As a result, the affairs of the barbershop radio and the seemingly transformed dominoes, neither heretofore reported, came to widespread public light. The local press took a dim view of both the discovery and the process:

> . . . While it is true that a series of unusual incidents have taken place over the better part of the past year, not only is there nothing to connect them, but also with a little digging beneath the surface, each of them can be easily explained. Far from preserving calm and public order, the commission's very existence has heightened anxieties

and legitimized essentially foolish concerns. And now, in implying that aliens have taken over the airways or that the devil himself has had a hand in a dominoes game, the politicians have once again sensationalized reports for their own purposes by playing to the most common denominators of fear and superstition.

Without subsequent disturbances, the filing of the report and its condemnation in the neighborhood weekly seemed to have been the last public words on the preceding series of irregularities. In private conversations, however, collective reference to the nine months of small wonders or to any of them individually continued to be made. At Mickens' barber shop, for instance, the opening strains of Rachmaninoff's prelude became both a kind of tonal greeting and a comic sign that someone had inappropriately changed the subject of conversation. Children on their way to or from school reminisced about the short-lived huts, passing the story to younger siblings who passed it on themselves. At Ramshead Park, the basketball crowd greeted shots that lacked style with raucous jeers of "Larr-y! Larr-y!" And among the populace at large there were random recollections or nonce remarks as well. "¿Recuerdas a la mujer con la gallina?" someone might say apropos of nothing. Or another, nudging his companion as they watched smoke billow from a burning building might jest, "Nah, dry ice."

Whether such memories or remarks rose to the level of lore is a difficult question. If the various episodes and their implied or putative significance were not fully absorbed into the neighborhood's culture, they at least maintained a lingering, if intangible, presence—hovering rather than penetrant. Perhaps it was much like the star above the Briscoe St. Baptist Church, weathered, begrimed, and rarely noticed but still undeniably there.

Selective Annotated Glossary

[For words omitted here see the prefatory note.]

Avrom. An Ashkenazic contraction of the Hebrew for Abraham.

Bimah. A raised platform standing before the ark housing the Torah scrolls and upon which is a desk used for reading from the Torah and conducting services. In orthodox tradition, the bimah and desk are in the center of the synagogue and the ark, at some distance, against or built into the wall before it.

Bris. The Jewish rite of circumcision.

Bubbe/Bobe. Grandmother.

Bomerke. Bum (f). Here with implications of sexual promiscuity.

Daven. Pray.

Erets Yisroel. The land of Israel.

Farputsing. Dressing up, dolling up—with implications of excess.

Farshteyst. Second person singular present tense of *farshteyn*. (Do you) understand?

Fartik. Done.

Fast forty days. Such a fast would have meant refraining from food and drink between sunrise and sunset.

Goy. Gentile.

Goylem. Golem. An automaton. A creature made of clay and infused with life, especially the one purportedly created by Rabbi Judah Loew of Prague in the 16th century C.E.

Grager. A ratcheted noisemaker used during the reading of the book of Esther on the festival of Purim to drown out the name of Haman, whose genocidal plot against the Jews in ancient Persia had been foiled.

Hamantashen. A three-cornered pastry eaten on Purim. (See *Grager* above.) The word literally means Haman's pockets, with folklore attributing the triangular shape variously to Haman's hat, ears, and the pockets themselves. A sweet consummation of the enemy in any case.

Horowitz-Margareten. A kosher foods company best known for its matzoh.

"If I am not for me, who will be for me, and if not now, when?" The character quotes Rabbi Hillel but omits a crucial sentence. The full quotation (allowing for variations among translators) should be: "If I am not for myself, who will be for me? If I am only for myself, what am I? And if not now, when?"

Kaddish. The word itself means "sanctification" and is part of the name of several variant prayers, most offered during synagogue services. The text here concerns the Mourner's Kaddish, recited during the prescribed period of mourning and subsequently at memorial services on specified holidays and on the anniversary of the decedent's death. However, as the character referring to it notes, the prayer makes no mention of death, and, praising the Holy Name throughout, is essentially an affirmation of faith. In the orthodox tradition, men are obliged to say the Mourner's Kaddish for deceased parents, spouses, siblings, and children. In more liberal traditions, women may undertake the same obligations.

Kashe. Kasha, buckwheat groats.

*Kashres (*Heb. *Kashrut).* Jewish dietary laws.

Khanuke. Chanukah/Hanukkah

*Kh'sidim (*pl.of *khosid).* Those who subscribe to the beliefs and practices of Hassidic Judaism.

Knish. A baked patty wrapped in dough and filled with various foodstuffs, but most prominently mashed potato and buckwheat groats (kasha).

Kol Nidre. The solemn liturgical declaration that introduces the evening service for the Day of Atonement.

L'khaim. To life.

Makhzor. A prayer book used for services on the New Year (Rosh Hashanah) and the Day of Atonement (Yom Kippur).

Mameloshn. The mother tongue; i.e. Yiddish.

Mazl tov. Good luck! A form of congratulation.

Matse. Unleavened bread. The spelling here reflects Yiddish pronunciation of "matzo(h)," or "matzah."

Meshuge. Insane, crazy, nuts.

Minyen. The quorum of ten adults required to hold a communal prayer service. Orthodox Judaism requires that the ten be males.

Mishpokhe. Extended family.

Mourner's Kaddish. See *Kaddish.*

Moyels [Anglicized pl. of moyel]. Those who perform ritual circumcision. See *Bris.*

Neshome ru. Rest for the soul. Here "rest" is conceived as synonymous with "peace" and the soul as it is present in the living.

Nu. An interjection capable of multiple meanings. For present purposes it may be translated as "so" or "well" if a question is implied or, otherwise, as a sign of reluctant acceptance as in "okay."

Nudzh/ing. Pester/ing.

Omeyn. Amen.

Pesakh. Passover.

Reb. Mister. A polite form of address when paired with a man's first name.

Sandek. A person (traditionally male) who is honored by holding the baby during his circumcision.

Shabes. The Sabbath.

Shalom bayit. Domestic peace. The phrase, however, typically refers to the relationship between a husband and wife rather than to that between a parent and child.

Shema. The first word of a prayer that is arguably the most central to Judaism. It is recited twice daily by observant Jews and at the approach of death. The opening line is translated as "Hear, O Israel: the Lord our God, the Lord is One." For additional information about the line and the prayer as a whole consult myjewishlearning.com and/or Chabad.org.

Shmates. Rags, but also applied dismissively and humorously to articles of clothing.

Shlemiel. Fool, bungler, jerk, etc.

Shofar. A ram's horn trumpet blown at various intervals during New Year (Rosh Hashanah) services and at the conclusion of the Day of Atonement (Yom Kippur).

Shtetelular. A coinage based on the Yiddish for "small town." In context, the word suggests that we need to place more emphasis on community and less on individuality.

Shul. Synagogue.

Shvartse. A black person. The word is often derogatory.

Sh'vues/Shavuot. The festival, seven weeks from the second day of Passover, commemorating the giving of the law to Moses at Mt. Sinai. It also celebrates the first harvest of the current year. (The first of these words reflects the Yiddish pronunciation of the Hebrew second word.)

Such a diamond is still a woman of worth. The speaker alludes in this passage to Proverbs 31:10.

Talis. Prayer shawl.

Tokhes. Behind, buttocks.

Tummlers. Noise makers.

Yarmulke. Skullcap.

Yasher koakh. A form of congratulation colloquially translated as "more power to you."

Yidishkayt. Jewish culture, traditions, practices or folkways which might or might not include religious observance.

Yortzeit. Anniversary of the deaths of specified family members upon which the Mourner's Kaddish (see *Kaddish* above) is recited.

Zeyde. Grandfather.

Acknowledgment

"The Labors of Leonard Vogel" appeared in *Jewish Fiction* (formerly called jewishfiction.net) #24 in 2020.